Hi, I'm JIMMY!

Like me, you probably noticed the world is run by adults.
But ask yourself: Who would do the best job
of making books that *kids* will love?

Yeah. **Kids!**

So that's how the idea of JIMMY books came to life.
We want every JIMMY book to be so good
that when you're finished, you'll say,

"PLEASE GIVE ME ANOTHER BOOK!"

Give this one a try and see if you agree.
(If not, you're probably an adult!)

JIMMY PATTERSON BOOKS
FOR YOUNG READERS

James Patterson Presents
Sci-Fi Junior High by John Martin and Scott Seegert
Sci-Fi Junior High: Crash Landing by John Martin and Scott Seegert
How to Be a Supervillain by Michael Fry
How to Be a Supervillain: Born to Be Good by Michael Fry
The Unflushables by Ron Bates
Ernestine, Catastrophe Queen by Merrill Wyatt

The Middle School Series by James Patterson
Middle School: The Worst Years of My Life
Middle School: Get Me Out of Here!
Middle School: Big Fat Liar
Middle School: How I Survived Bullies, Broccoli, and Snake Hill
Middle School: Ultimate Showdown
Middle School: Save Rafe!
Middle School: Just My Rotten Luck
Middle School: Dog's Best Friend
Middle School: Escape to Australia
Middle School: From Hero to Zero

The I Funny Series by James Patterson
I Funny
I Even Funnier
I Totally Funniest
I Funny TV
I Funny: School of Laughs
The Nerdiest, Wimpiest, Dorkiest I Funny Ever

The Treasure Hunters Series by James Patterson
Treasure Hunters
Treasure Hunters: Danger Down the Nile

Treasure Hunters: Secret of the Forbidden City
Treasure Hunters: Peril at the Top of the World
Treasure Hunters: Quest for the City of Gold

The House of Robots Series by James Patterson
House of Robots
House of Robots: Robots Go Wild!
House of Robots: Robot Revolution

The Daniel X Series by James Patterson
The Dangerous Days of Daniel X
Daniel X: Watch the Skies
Daniel X: Demons and Druids
Daniel X: Game Over
Daniel X: Armageddon
Daniel X: Lights Out

Other Illustrated Novels and Stories
Not So Normal Norbert
Laugh Out Loud
Pottymouth and Stoopid
Jacky Ha-Ha
Jacky Ha-Ha: My Life Is a Joke
Public School Superhero
Word of Mouse
Give Please a Chance
Give Thank You a Try
Big Words for Little Geniuses
Cuddly Critters for Little Geniuses
The Candies Save Christmas

For exclusives, trailers, and other information,
visit jimmypatterson.org.

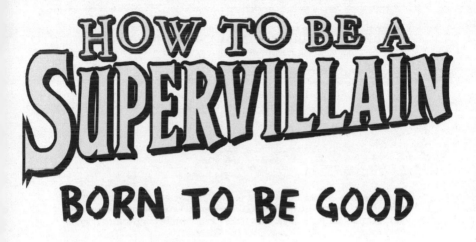

HOW TO BE A SUPERVILLAIN

BORN TO BE GOOD

Michael Fry

JIMMY Patterson Books

LITTLE, BROWN AND COMPANY

New York Boston London

Copyright © 2018 by Michael Fry
Excerpt of *How to Be a Supervillain* copyright © 2017 by Michael Fry

Hachette Book Group supports the right to free expression and the value of copyright. The purpose of copyright is to encourage writers and artists to produce the creative works that enrich our culture.

The scanning, uploading, and distribution of this book without permission is a theft of the author's intellectual property. If you would like permission to use material from the book (other than for review purposes), please contact permissions@hbgusa.com. Thank you for your support of the author's rights.

JIMMY Patterson Books / Little, Brown and Company
Hachette Book Group
1290 Avenue of the Americas, New York, NY 10104
jimmypatterson.org

First Edition: May 2018

JIMMY Patterson Books is an imprint of Little, Brown and Company, a division of Hachette Book Group, Inc. The Little, Brown name and logo are trademarks of Hachette Book Group, Inc. The JIMMY Patterson Books® name and logo are trademarks of JBP Business, LLC.

The publisher is not responsible for websites (or their content) that are not owned by the publisher.

The Hachette Speakers Bureau provides a wide range of authors for speaking events. To find out more, go to hachettespeakersbureau.com or call (866) 376-6591.

Library of Congress Cataloguing-in-Publication Data
Names: Fry, Michael, 1959- author, illustrator.
Title: Born to Be Good / Michael Fry.
Description: First edition. | New York: Little, Brown and Company, 2018. | Series: How to Be a Supervillain; 2 | "JIMMY Patterson Books." | Summary: "Twelve-year-old do-gooder Victor Spoil, a disappointment to his supervillain parents, must save the world from an evil scheme to enslave the superheroes and villains."
Identifiers: LCCN 2018003926 | ISBN 978-0-316-31915-7 (hc) Subjects: | CYAC: Supervillains—Fiction. | Superheroes—Fiction. | Identity—Fiction. | Humorous stories. | BISAC: JUVENILE FICTION / Action & Adventure / General. | COMICS & GRAPHIC NOVELS / Superheroes. | JUVENILE FICTION / Comics & Graphic Novels / Superheroes. | JUVENILE FICTION / Humorous Stories. | JUVENILE FICTION / Family / General (see also headings under Social Issues).
Classification: LCC PZ7.F9234 Bo 2018 | DDC [Fic]—dc23 LC record available at https://lccn.loc.gov/2018003926

10 9 8 7 6 5 4 3 2 1

LSC-H

Printed in the United States of America

To Neva

HOW TO BE A SUPERVILLAIN

BORN TO BE GOOD

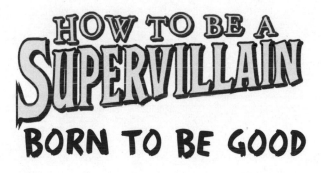

PROLOGUE

So, you want to be a supervillain?

Let's start with the basics. Let's start with the costume.

A good supervillain costume is comfortable yet intimidating. In other words, never too saggy in the butt.

Inflatable muscles are allowed, but be careful not to overinflate.

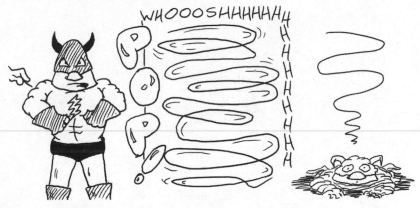

Capes are fine. Just make sure they're not too long.

Next up is the action pose. Every supervillain has a signature action pose. An action pose demonstrates strength and determination.

Don't forget your evil laugh. It's got to be scary. And creepy. But not too creepy.

Supervillains with allergies, lung conditions, or over fifty should avoid the evil laugh.

4

After you've got your action pose and your evil laugh down, it's time to work on your supervillain monologue. A monologue is a long-winded speech about how you're so evil, how you're going to take over the world, and what exactly you're going to do to the superhero.

The monologue should be long, but not too long.

Last, but not least, is your superpower. There are cool superpowers.

And there are lame superpowers.

That's it! You now have all the tools to take over the world as a Serious, Truly Evil, Thoroughly Bad, Absolutely Rotten Supervillain.

Just like me!

I should explain.

CHAPTER 1

It's good to be bad.

No. Seriously. It is.

That's what I learned when I defeated Dr. Deplorable and saved the world.

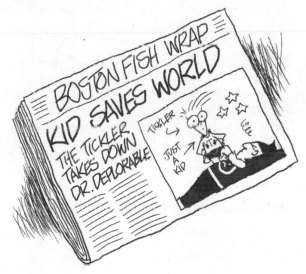

Yeah. *That* happened.

I, Victor Spoil, a junior supervillain from a long line of supervillains, six months ago SAVED THE WORLD!

Which is a good deed. Done by a bad kid. Confused? Me too.

You see, this whole good vs. evil thing is just a show we supers put on for the public. We dress up in tights and capes and pretend to battle.

Why do we pretend? Because years ago things got *way* out of hand (destruction, mayhem, using buses as dodge balls)...

...and we all agreed to cool it. Or, more accurately, the Authority made us cool it. The Authority has real power, the power to shoot a super into space if he/she doesn't toe the line.

This arrangement worked. For a while. At least until Dr. Deplorable decided he wanted to be a real supervillain and take over the world.

But I stopped him. With some help from my parents, the Spoil Sports, and my mentor, the Smear.

So when it really counted and lives were at stake, the whole good vs. evil thing broke down. And someone had to do the *right* thing. And that someone was me.

Yeah. I'm the Tickler. I know, pretty lame. But hey, it worked!

But that was six months ago. Six months is a long time in the super business. Things change. People forget.

People get mean,

CHAPTER 2

Meet Niles. He's the big (dumb) kid on campus here at Junior Super Academy. But he thinks he's God's gift to junior superheroes.

HANDSOME →
CONFIDENT →
REAL CHIN →
ACTUAL SHOULDERS →
PINE FRESH SCENT →
+ BRITISH ACCENT →

TOTAL BUTT-HEAD →

CHEERS, MATE!

Ever since I started at JSA he's been a pain in my spleen. So far, I've been able to ignore him.

I mean, he's never really been any competition.
Until now...

How can Octavia like him? She was there when I took down Dr. Deplorable. She had my back. I had her back. We were back backers from way back. And here she was giggling and smiling at this...this...this...superjerk.

How could she?

"Mr. Spoil?" asked a distant nasal drone. "Mr. Spoil, are you with us?"

"Huh?" I said, as I slowly turned from staring at Octavia and Niles to my Trash-Talking 101 instructor, Mr. Stupendous.

Crap! I hadn't done the reading. Well, I'd done lots of *other* reading. I'd read all about toads. Super interesting. I'd read *How to Build an Igloo*. Trickier than you'd think. I'd read a biography of Nikola Tesla. Edison gets all the attention, but Tesla was the real genius. I'd read lots of stuff. I love to read.

But I hadn't done the class reading.

So I had no idea what the number one most important principle in trash-talking was.

I ventured, "Never let them see you pee your pants?"

The class laughed. Hey, it was a good guess.

"No," said Mr. Stupendous. "Anyone else?"

Niles raised his hand. "When they go low, you go subterranean."

Mr. Stupendous smiled. "Yes. Excellent. Thank you, Niles."

Niles shot me a bask-in-my-glorious-presence-you-dull-hopeless-loser-you grin.

I shot him back an eat-hot-death-you-miserable-loathsome-butt-hat grin.

TOXIC GRIN-OFF

Mr. Stupendous continued, "The key to trash-talking is to get your opponents off balance. To get in their heads. To make them hesitate. Doubt. Stumble. Make a mistake. And the way to do that is to go low, really low, so low that they have to look up to look down.

"This is more than insults, people. You're look-ing for a permanent stain on their souls. It's not enough to say, 'Your mother wears last season's nonstandard arch-supported corrective insoles that she buys at the Dollar Store from the five-for-a-dollar bin.' That's a pinprick. A mosquito bite. You need to go deeper. You need to rip and tear. You need to make it hurt. You need to go full Komodo dragon on their butts."

Komodo dragons? Are they even known for their vicious insults? I wasn't sure. Maybe. Still, was I the only one who thought this was all a tad excessive? I looked around. I caught Octavia's rolling eyes. Cool. I wasn't alone.

Mr. Stupendous continued, "Who would like to come to the front of the class and demonstrate? Niles? Mr. Spoil?"

Groan. I hate going to the front of the class. There's just too much at risk. Your fly could be down. You could have a third-eye-sized zit in the middle of your forehead. You might fart. It's not the trash-talking. I can do that. It's the potential global humiliation that comes with putting your twelve-year-old not-ready-for-prime-time self out there for all the world to mock.

Mr. Stupendous stared at us. "Gentlemen?"

Niles and I got up and approached the front of the class. Niles was grinning. He thought he had me. He thought he could out-insult me.

He was wrong.

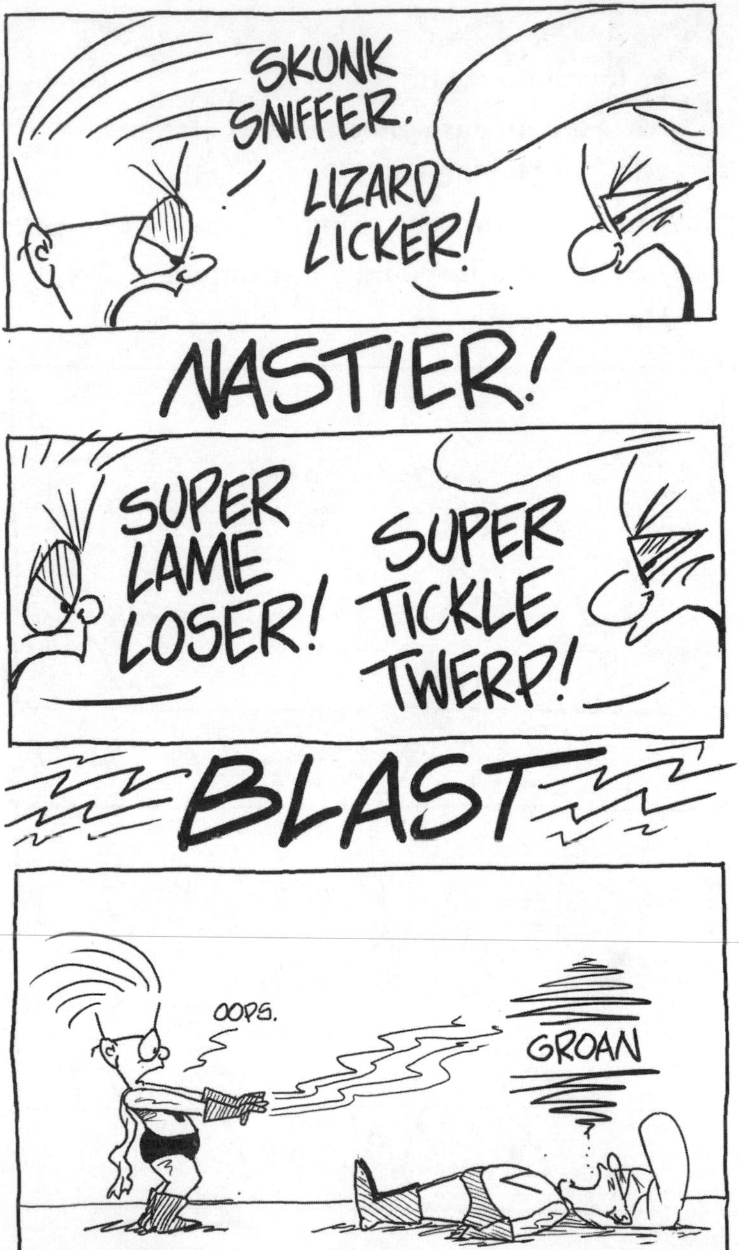
SKUNK SNIFFER.
LIZARD LICKER!
NASTIER!
SUPER LAME LOSER!
SUPER TICKLE TWERP!
BLAST
OOPS.
GROAN

CHAPTER 3

"What was *that?*" cried Mr. Stupendous.

"Sorry," I muttered.

Niles pointed at me. "That kid is dangerous! He almost..."

"I wouldn't..." I said.

Mr. Stupendous stared hard at me. "You almost did."

"I just tickled him," I said.

Niles sat up. "...TO DEATH!"

I rolled my eyes. "You're fine."

I looked around the room. All the kids looked scared....

... OF ME?

GULP

"He's fine," I said. "Things just got a little, you know, out of hand."

Niles stood up. "You're a menace, Spoil! You're not a supervillain. You're not a superhero. You're just a jerk!"

I looked around the class again. Octavia was staring at me. She slowly shook her head.

I tried to explain. "Look, it was an accident. It won't happen again. I promise. I wouldn't ever hurt anyone. Well, I mean, anyone who didn't deserve it. Sure, Niles is annoying. You all know that. He insulted me. He..."

"Got in your head," said Mr. Stupendous. "He got you to make a mistake. He got you to lose your cool. He got you to..."

"Forget who I am," I said, as Niles grinned his snot-eating grin.

Mr. Stupendous pointed. "To the Penalty Cave, Spoil!"

"No!" I protested. "Not the Penalty Cave!"

I hate the Penalty Cave. It's got bugs. And bats. And it smells like old supersocks.

"Now!" yelled Mr. Stupendous.

I slunk off. Out of the corner of my eye I could

see Octavia. She looked worried. Or maybe it was just pity. Hard to tell the difference when you're feeling sorry for yourself.

The Penalty Cave is across from the Cafetorium, next to the garbage cans and the recycling. The walk to the Penalty Cave is a walk of shame. It goes past all the classrooms. Everyone can see you. Everyone can see you screwed up big-time. Everyone feels comfort in the fact that it's me walking to the Penalty Cave—and not them.

You're welcome, everyone.

I entered the Penalty Cave and sat down. A bug skittered up a rock. I swear it looked at me and said...

LOSER.

CHAPTER 4

Hero to zero in six short months. Must be some kind of record. Fortunately, back in my room, I had just the book to look that up.

GUINNESS BOOK OF WORLD RECORDS

NOPE. SOMEONE ELSE DID IT IN FOUR MONTHS.

GUINNESS BOOK OF WORLD...

Nope. Can't even manage that.

I put the book away with all my other books (did I mention I like to read?) and lay back on my bed.

"What am I going to do?" I asked the ceiling.

But the ceiling didn't answer. It never does. Stupid ceiling.

The door opened and a large shadow fell over me.

It was my roommate, Javy. Javy has issues judging personal space. As in, he doesn't bother.

"Javy, what did we talk about?" I said.

"What? Too close?" asked Javy.

"Way too close."

I pointed to his bed. "Sit over there, Javy."

He nodded. "Right."

Javy is a good kid. Weird, but good. Sweet, even. He's a junior superhero. His power is reading minds. Kind of. Sort of. Not really. He's working on it.

"You're thinking you blew it with Octavia today," said Javy.

Maybe he's getting better.

"Yes. But no. I'm thinking what's the point of this whole supercircus?"

"Free costumes!"

"There's more to life than free costumes, Javy."

"We're training to be entertainers. We make civilians happy."

"As they watch us fake-beat the snot out of each other."

"It wasn't fake when you took down Dr. Deplorable."

"That was a onetime thing. It'll never happen again. Basically, we supers are useless."

"Hey, I'm not useless."

"Of course not. I didn't mean..."

"There was that one time I read Patty's mind and I knew right away she wouldn't go to the dance with me. That's not useless."

"You have a useful power, Javy," I said. "Me? I tickle people."

"You make people laugh."

"Completely against their will. And until they think they're going to explode."

"Niles needed to laugh."

"Not that hard."

The door burst open.

WHO'S OUR BAD BOY?!

SLAM!

27

Groan. I completely forgot it was Parents Weekend.

I sighed. "Hi, Mom and Dad."

"What's this?" said Mom. "Is this some attitude I'm seeing?"

Dad nodded. "He's not happy to see us. He looks *super* irritated."

Mom looked at Dad. Dad looked at Mom. Then they both looked at me. And smiled. Sort of. As I've explained in the past, they don't use those muscles very often.

"He gets that from me," said Mom.

"I'm so proud," added Dad.

I rolled over and faced the wall. "Please go away," I said.

"He's snubbing us!" said Dad.

"Wait till I tell the girls at CrossFit!" said Mom.

"Wait till I tell the guys at the Donut Palace!" said Dad.

Mom glared at Dad.

Dad said, "Did I say that out loud?"

I sighed.

"If you put half the energy you spend eating donuts toward exercising, you could tie your own shoes," said Mom.

I moaned. "Mom? Please?"

"I like it when you tie my shoes," said Dad. "You do the loops just right. They never come untied."

"Dad, c'mon!" I cried.

Mom eyed Dad. "One of these days, I'm going to tie them in *triple* knots and then I'm going to run off to Fiji and you'll never get them untied!"

"Fiji?" said Dad. "Gee, who has a secret lair in Fiji? Could it be the Prince of Pandemonium?"

"Guys!" I shouted.

Mom rolled her eyes. "We're just friends. When are you going to let that go?"

"Friends," said Dad. "Ha! I saw the way you touched his cheek at VillainCon last year."

"There was *acid* on his cheek!" yelled Mom. "He bumped into that leaky Sulfuric Boy. He could have been badly burned!"

"A likely story," snorted Dad.

"ENOUGH!" I screamed. "GO! AWAY! NOW!"

My parents stared at me.

"I like the bad attitude," said Dad.

Mom added, "Yes. But save it for the festivities. Tomorrow's a big day. Don't go to bed too early."

"Yes," said Dad. "And don't forget to forget to floss."

And then, finally, they left.

CHAPTER 5

"Who can tell me the factors that led to the Super Revolution of 1957?" asked Dr. Comet Head.

It was the next day and I was in Super World History class. Or, as I like to call it, Advanced Snoozefest.

I bolted awake. "Wait? What?"
The class laughed.

At me.

Not *with* me.

Dr. Comet Head glared. "Now that you're so well rested perhaps you can elucidate us all with your vast knowledge of the causes of the Super Revolution of 1957, including, but not limited to, taxation, regulation, and the rise of the Authority."

I yawned. "The Super Revolution of 1957 came about after a long period of super frustration with civilian authority over superbattle taxes and unnecessary overregulation of superpowers. The resulting superprotest decimated downtown Pittsburgh and led to the Truce and joint super/civilian governing Authority we have today. Which led to fake, scripted battles, blah, blah, blah, and fake superheroes and supervillains, blah, blah, blah."

See. I know stuff.

"You're the only fake super around here," said Niles from the back of the class.

"Oooooooooooh!" taunted the class.

"Settle down," said Dr. Comet Head.

I stood up and turned around. Niles and Octavia were sitting at the back of the class next to each other.

I said, "You're absolutely right, Niles. I'm a fake junior super. The only difference between you and me is that I know it and you don't."

The class let loose with another, "Oooooooooooh!"

Niles stood up, raised his arm, and...

A plasma blast seems pretty dangerous, but it's not. Annoying? Sure. Kind of like being hit in the chest by a seagull. Unpleasant and kinda itchy, but really no big deal. Nothing compared to my tickle power.

"Boys!" yelled Dr. Comet Head. "No battling in class! You know the rules!"

"Get up, freak!" yelled Niles. "I can take you. Not like last time when you surprised me!"

Despite my superpower advantage, I just lay there.

This was so getting old. I realized that I just didn't care that much. I didn't care about battling Niles. I didn't care about Super World History. I didn't care about Trash-Talking 101. I really didn't care about Parents Weekend. The only thing I did care about was...

I DON'T WANT TO DO THIS ANYMORE.

"What?" said Niles.

"I don't want to be a super anymore."

The class gasped.

Octavia stage-whispered, "Victor! You don't mean that!"

"Yes. Yes, I do," I said.

There was a beat of silence.

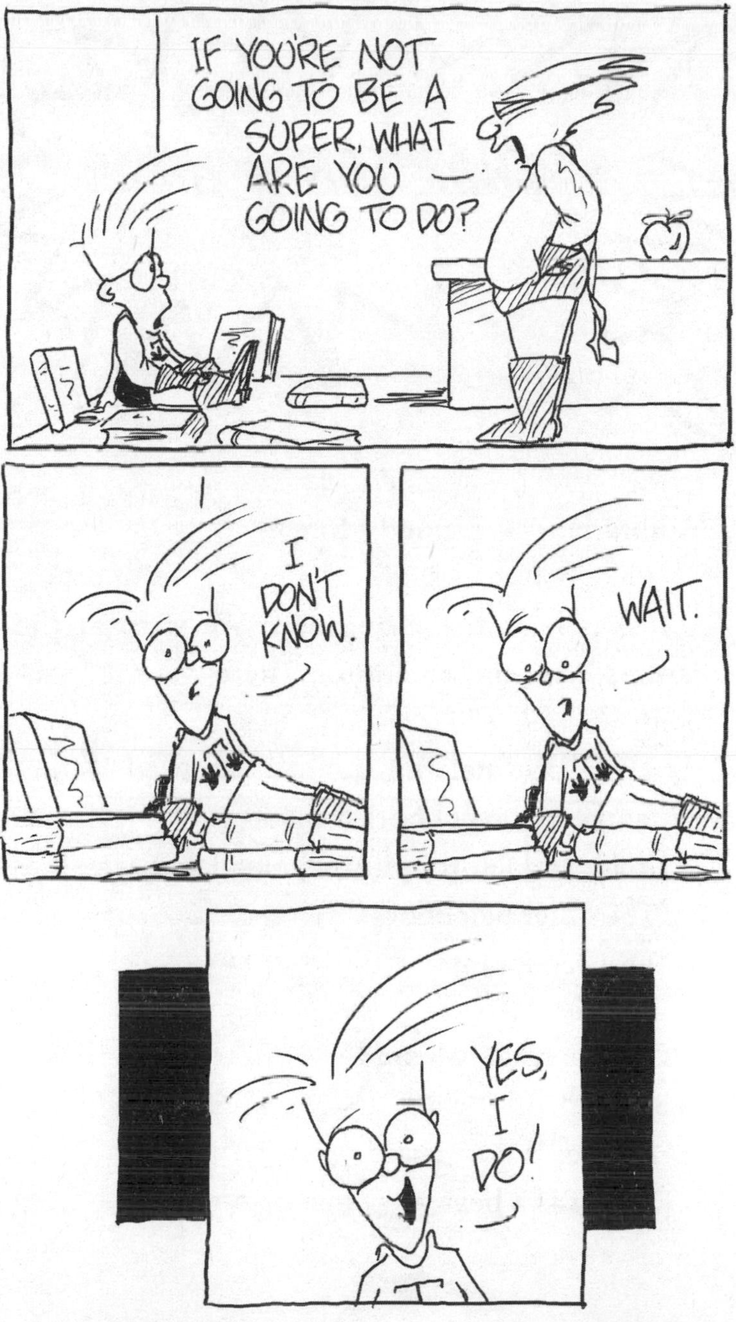
IF YOU'RE NOT GOING TO BE A SUPER, WHAT ARE YOU GOING TO DO?
I DON'T KNOW.
WAIT.
YES, I DO!

CHAPTER **6**

"A librarian?" screamed Mom.

"I like books," I said.

It was later that afternoon. We were at the Parents Weekend reception. There were refreshments and pie. I like pie.

"That's beside the point!" growled Mom. "What will the neighbors think?"

I said, "I don't think Anvil Head will care."

"The other neighbors!"

"Dr. Deodorant?"

FRESH PINE SCENT

DR. DEODORANT

MAKES STUFF SMELL GOOD

"You know what I mean," said Mom.

Actually, I had no idea what she meant. All I knew is that I was bored with the whole super thing and wanted out.

Dad walked up with a plate full of pie.

"Your son wants to be a librarian," said Mom.

"No, he doesn't," said Dad, in between bites. "He's just messing with us because that's what budding supervillains do."

"I'm not messing with you," I said.

Dad continued, "And then they lie about it."

Mom bought it. "I'm so relieved."

I shook my head. "I'm not lying."

But they weren't listening. They never listen.

Javy ran up, looking panicked. "Victor, my parents are missing."

"Your parents are invisible. They're always missing," I pointed out.

"Not like this," said Javy. "Even if I can't see them, I can always find them by the smell of Dad's cologne."

INVISIBLE DAD

MAX BODY SPRAY (TANGERINE AND LAVA SCENT)

SNIFF-SNIFF

POPS?

Javy shook his head. "I can't smell him any-where."

I said, "I'm sure they'll turn up."

Javy walked off, sniffing as he went.

"Victor!" yelled a familiar voice.

It was Octavia's mom, one half of the super-hero team called the Sparkles. She was standing with Mr. Sparkle and Octavia.

OVER HERE!!

SPARKLES

SPARKLES

"Hey, Mr. and Mrs. Sparkle," I said. "Hey, Octavia."

"Hey," grumbled Octavia.

Mr. Sparkle cheered, "My, you've grown!"

"It's only been six months," I said.

"No, you're grimmer. Have you been working on your scowl?" asked Mrs. Sparkle.

"No more than usual," I answered.

"Victor thinks this whole super thing is silly," said Octavia. "He wants to quit."

"Quit?" said Mr. Sparkle. "You can't quit. You saved the world!"

"I got lucky," I said.

"Modesty in a supervillain?" said Mrs. Sparkle. "It's not very becoming."

I said, "Look, that was a onetime thing."

"You never know," said Mr. Sparkle. "Heroes and villains will surprise you. We need someone with a level head like yours."

"Yes," said Niles, from behind us. "What would we do without good old levelheaded Victor? Hero of the Bostocalypse. Savior of the Truce. The Mad Tickler! The Big Bad Tickling *Librarian!*"

See. Now even Octavia was laughing at me. Remind me again. Why did I want to continue doing this super thing?

CHAPTER 7

It's the Smear! He's here! Never fear! He's holding root beer!

I'll stop now.

"What are you doing here?" I asked.

"I was in the neighborhood," he said. "Thought I'd see what my favorite junior supervillain was up to."

"You're here for the pie, aren't you?" I asked.

The Smear leaned down and whispered, "Of course I'm here for the pie."

I smiled. The Smear smiled. Good times.

A few months ago, the Smear took me on as an apprentice when no one else would. He showed me the super ropes. He taught me how to villain.

The most important thing he taught me was that good and evil are two sides of the same coin. You can't have one without the other. And when you make them work together, you can do anything.

You know, like save the world. The thing that made me a hero until people realized I was just me. Someone who's good at tickling.

"I hear you want to quit," said the Smear, as we headed to the pie table.

"The world doesn't need saving anymore," I pointed out.

"For now."

"For now?"

The Smear cut himself a slice of pie, then pointed to a nearby supervillain. "Stuff happens. One day you're fake-fighting Moldy Dave and the next day Moldy Dave decides to take over the world."

SERIOUSLY?

THE STINK IS STRONG IN THIS ONE.

DRIP DRIP

I rolled my eyes. "I think the world is safe from Moldy Dave."

The Smear took a bite of pie. "Maybe. But what if he gets bit by a radioactive tick and starts to crave moose blood?"

"And what if he sleepwalks through a car wash and is no longer moldy?"

"Exactly my point. *Anything* can happen. And usually does. And it never quite turns out the way you think."

"Why is it my responsibility to keep moose safe from Moldy Dave?"

"You're special, kid," said the Smear. "You proved that in Boston."

"But I don't want to be special," I said. "I want to be a librarian."

"It doesn't work like that. You're special whether you want to be or not. Your only choice is whether to use your gift."

"Gift? I tickle people."

"You know the rules," said the Smear. "You don't choose your power, it chooses you."

I rolled my eyes. "That's a stupid rule."

The Smear shook his head. "Dude, I stain people."

"Exactly my point. We're a joke!"

The Smear grabbed me by the shoulders and looked me in the eye. "Victor, listen to me very carefully. It's not the superpower, it's *the power of the super*."

"What does that even mean?"

"I've known supers with tremendous powers who couldn't find their butt with two hands and a map."

"Yeah, so?"

"You can find your butt."

"*That's* my special skill?"

He didn't answer because we were interrupted by the new president of the Junior Super Academy.

"Attention students, parents, and significant supers...

...WELCOME TO JUNIOR SUPER ACADEMY!

I said, "Wait, is that Norman? Norman from the Authority?"

The Smear whispered. "No way. This guy's too calm. Too relaxed. Too…"

"…Norman."

CHAPTER 8

Norman used to work for the Authority. A somewhat nervous sort, he tried to stage-manage our fake superbattles.

Tried. And failed.

Now he's the new president of the Junior Super Academy.

Seems like kind of a downgrade.

"Welcome, students and parents of the Junior Super Academy," said Norman. "It is my distinct honor to address you today as your new president and Super Rules instructor."

Super Rules is my worst class. So many rules. So little sense.

Norman continued. "Junior Super Academy is at a crossroads. We have served the super community for years by sending graduates to perform for all civilians. We honor the Truce with the Authority by limiting superdamage and fighting only in scripted matches. We get to fight. No one gets hurt. No one gets banished into space."

The Smear whispered, "Yet."

Norman went on. "But after the events six months ago with Dr. Deplorable, we need to take stock. We need to reaffirm our commitment to the Truce. All of us need to keep a careful eye on our fellow supers in order to ferret out those who may harbor resentment and therefore do us all harm."

"One way we can commit to maintaining the Truce is by raising our standards. We *are* entertainers, after all, and it is by entertaining civilians that we ensure our safe, secure, and happy superfuture."

Norman droned on. "The best way to ensure our future is to invest in it. That's why I'm proud to announce several new capital improvements, starting with the Dr. Leadfoot Memorial Shark Tank."

"We've also completely refurbished the Mr. Cyclops Memorial Laser Lab."

"And we've completely endowed a new chair in the GigaGopher Memorial School of Secret Lair Architecture."

In case it wasn't obvious, supers are quite accident-prone.

"Of course," said Norman. "We can't continue these projects unless everyone chips in to our capital improvement drive.

The Scratchys are known for pledging big and never following through.

Norman continued, "As I look out on this crowd of young, budding supers and their families, I can see that the superfuture is bright and that our role in distracting civilians from their boring, mundane lives is secure. So, it is with great pleasure that I—"

Norman was interrupted by Javy walking behind him across the stage. Walking and sniffing.

CHAPTER 9

"I can't smell them anywhere," said Javy.

"Your parents will turn up," I said. "They always do."

It was later that night back in our dorm room.

Javy looked at me. "I'm worried. I don't want them to miss out on tomorrow."

Tomorrow was the Junior Super Exhibition, where all the students demonstrated their new superskills for their parents.

Or lack thereof.

"We'll find your parents in the morning," I said. "I'm sure they're fine."

"Oh, I nearly forgot," said Javy, as he reached into his pocket. "Octavia gave me this to give you."

He handed me a note.

I sighed, "She's just going to try to talk me out of quitting."

"C'mon, you're not really going to quit," said Javy.

"Yes. I am."

"No. You're not."

"Watch me."

"I'm watching."

I said, "I mean, I'm not going to do it right this second."

"Why not?" said Javy. "No one's stopping you."

"I'm going to do it. You know, when I'm ready."

"No time like the present."

"Okay, fine. I quit."

Javy shook his head. "You can't. You have to go through processing. There's paperwork. Then they wipe your memory of all stuff super."

"That's not true."

"It is. Remember the Taco Kid? Squirted hot salsa out of his eyes? He quit. Said he was tired of crying all the time. I saw him the other day, working at Scarbucks. He didn't recognize me. He even wrote my name on my cup wrong."

I said, "You're making this up."

"Maybe," said Javy. "But are you willing to take that risk? You'd forget about all this junior super stuff. You'd forget about you. You'd forget about *me!*"

"I could never forget about you, Javy."

"Because I'm your best friend and you'd be lost without me?"

"That, and you're super annoying."

"Yes!" smiled Javy. "I may read minds for a living, but I'm also really good at irritating them, too."

"Super good."

Javy looked at me. "I'd also be lost at school without you."

"You'd do fine without me."

"Maybe. But I really don't want to find out."

I sighed. "Fine. I'll go see Octavia."

Javy raised his arms in triumph. "Yay! I wore you down."

"You're good at that."

"I read minds, I'm annoying, and I'm persistent. I have *all* the superpowers. Now, let's go."

"I have to brush my teeth first."

"Seriously?"

"Oral hygiene is the foundation of supervillainry."

"Aren't supervillains supposed to have bad breath?"

CHAPTER 10

Javy and I met Octavia at the Academy Playscape.
The Junior Supervillain Academy Playscape is
not your normal playscape. It's kind of extreme.

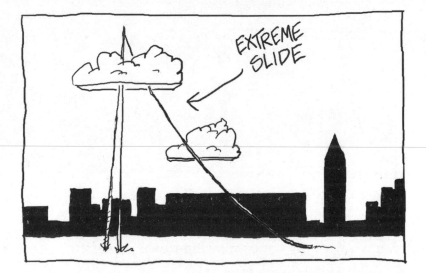

EXTREME
SLIDE

"I wasn't sure you'd come," said Octavia.

"He didn't want to," said Javy. "But I wore him down with my super-wearing-down powers."

I nodded. "Yes. He did."

"I want to talk you out of quitting," said Octavia.

I said, "I figured."

"We need you," said Octavia. "Even though you're annoying and can be a jerk sometimes."

"Gee, thanks," I said.

"You're not like the other superkids," said Octavia.

I rolled my eyes. "I know. I've heard. I'm special."

"You *are* special!" said Octavia. "You saved the world. You know, with some help."

I said, "I just did what any highly motivated kid with freakish tickling superskills would do."

"No," said Octavia. "You did more. You did a lot more. More than you had to."

"Maybe," I said. "But it doesn't matter. No one cares. We live in a what-have-you-done-for-me-lately world. The Bostocalypse was only six months ago. But it could have been sixty years for all anyone cares. Look, I did it. It's over. Time to move on."

Octavia looked down, "I care. You didn't just save the world. You saved me."

Javy added, "And me."

"No," I protested. "That's not what I meant. What I meant is—"

WHAT HE MEANS IS, IT'S ALL ABOUT HIM. NO ONE CARES ABOUT HIM. NO ONE IDOLIZES HIM. NO ONE REMEMBERS **HIM!!**

I cried, "No!"

Niles walked up to Octavia. "This is what I was trying to tell you. At the end of the day, he's just a selfish jerk."

I scowled. "Said the selfish-er jerk."

"I don't think *selfish-er* is a word," said Javy.

Niles laughed. "Yeah, a librarian should know that. Guess you're going to fail at that, too."

Octavia yelled. "STOP IT! ALL OF YOU!"

We stopped.

"Things got out of hand the other day," said Octavia. "The two of you need to apologize."

"To who?!" said both Niles and me.

Niles pointed at me. "He almost tickled me to death."

"You're exaggerating," I said.

Niles raised his shirt.

CRASH BANG OOF!

"I've had it with both of you!" yelled Octavia.

Octavia stalked off. "Superboys. Idiots in training capes."

"I should finish you off!" barked Niles. "One more plasma blast would do it. But you're leaving anyway, so I'll spare you so you can feel your shame day in and day out. You're welcome!"

Okay, first of all, only super*villains* are supposed to monologue. Second of all, as I've said, there's no way his plasma blasts would hurt me. They're no match for my tickle surge. You know, when I'm not wrapped around a swing set.

Niles wasn't done monologuing. "You're finished, Tickle Boy. You're right! No one cares what you did at the Bostocalypse. No one will remember. Go on, become a librarian! Become a nobody! Become a—"

MOUSE-
PILOTED STAIN
BOMBER

HEE!
HEE!
HEE!

STICKY-GOO
BOMB*

* ON TOP
OF GLITTER
BOMB

?

The Smear stepped out of the shadows. "I thought he'd never shut up."

I said, "I had everything under control."

Before I could explain, every cell phone in the Academy went off at the same time.

My phone was blasting a Missing-Super Alert.
"Who's missing now?" I asked.

CHAPTER 11

Every light in the Academy came on at once. Superkids spilled out of their dorms. They were all staring at their phones. And their phones all said the same thing.

MISSING
MULLET MAN
THE HOARDER
TOE NAIL GUY
DR. GLOOM
MS. FLUSTERED
ANXIETY DUDE
THE FLASHING BLINKER!
GECKO GAL

Every superparent was missing. Including...

Javy cried, "*All* the supers are missing! Not just my parents! I'm not crazy!"

"Still a little crazy," I said.

"But a good kind of crazy," said Javy. "Not the sad kind of crazy where people laugh at you when your invisible parents go missing."

I agreed. "The good kind of crazy."

Octavia said, "What happened? Where are all the grownup supers? Where's Norman?"

"I'm right here," said Norman, as he walked out of the shadows. "And everything's under control. Just remain calm. Like me."

Okay, so much for Norman.

"Not all the grownup supers are missing," said the Smear, as he appeared with Moldy Dave in tow.

PRESENT!

"I found him wandering around in the dark," said the Smear. "Well, actually I smelled him first. Then I found the slime trail. Then I found Moldy Dave."

"There was a bright light," muttered Moldy Dave. "Then I was on a table. There was a *huge* needle. I don't remember anything after that."

"ALIENS!" screamed Javy.

"Wait a second," said the Smear. "What was the last movie you saw?"

"*Saturn Seeks Schnauzers,*" said Moldy Dave.

"I liked the story, but the computer-generated schnauzers were completely unbelievable," he added.

The Smear nodded. "You imagined all this. I suspect you passed out from your mildew secretions and had a bad dream."

"I'm so relieved!" cried Javy. "I *hate* needles."

"But it was all so real," said Moldy Dave. "It smelled like tangerines. Tangerines and...

... LAVA.

DAD!

CHAPTER 12

Oh. Hang on. You're probably wondering what happened to Niles. He's fine. He's encased in goo from the Smear's sticky goo bomb. He can see and hear everything, but he can't move or speak.

We'll release him.

STICKY GOO

GRUMBLE GRUMBLE

Eventually.

Okay, back to Moldy Dave's weird story.

The Smear looked around. "Who can read minds?"

Javy slowly raised his hand. "I read minds...

...BUT I'M DYSLEXIC.

TERRIFIC.

Javy explained, "I can read minds, but sometimes I get stuff mixed up. Like that time I read my mom's mind and thought she wanted me to hand her a banana. But she really wanted me to clean my room. You know, that kind of thing."

The Smear closed his eyes. "Anyone else?"

No one else raised their hand.

"Fine, Javy," sighed the Smear. "Give it a shot."

Javy laid his hands on Moldy Dave. He closed his eyes. Then a look of confusion crossed his face.

"Get on with it!" yelled the Smear.

"Okay, okay," muttered Javy. He described what he saw in Moldy Dave's memories.

...TOWARD A SHIP. A BIG SHIP. LIKE A GIANT SQUID. OR AN OCTOPUS. OR MAYBE A LARGE GOLDFISH. IT'S THE DYSLEXIA! I CAN'T TELL.

THEN HE ENTERS THE SHIP AND... OH, MY GOD!

CHAPTER 13

Javy's eyes were closed. But his mouth was open. Wide open.

"It's everyone!" he cried. "Mom! Dad! The Spoil Sports! The Sparklers! All the supers. They're all there!"

"I'm not there," said Moldy Dave.

"Yes," said the Smear. "We noticed that."

"They're where?" I asked.

"They're on the ship. Stacked on shelves."

"Are they dead?" asked Moldy Dave.

"No. I don't think so," said Javy. "They're frozen. Frozen in action poses."

The Smear said, "It sounds like suspended animation."

"What?" I asked.

"They're alive, but they're frozen in place. They're prisoners."

"Why did I get sent back here?" asked Moldy Dave.

"They didn't want you," said the Smear.

Moldy Dave thought for a second. "They only wanted the cool supers?"

The Smear shrugged. "They didn't want me, either."

"Or any of us junior supers," I added.

"Hmm," said the Smear. "They're frozen in action poses. They're action figures!"

Octavia said, "It's almost like someone is...I don't know...*collecting* them?"

"But not the lame ones," Moldy Dave pouted.

I said, "Like us?"

CHAPTER 14

I couldn't move. The tractor beam had me and was slowly pulling me...up.

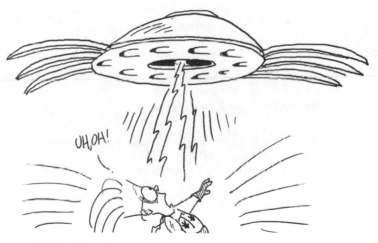

UH,OH!

"HELP!" I screamed.

Then I felt a hand on my foot. Then another hand. I looked down.

The Smear had me. He was hanging on. Pulling me back to Earth. Then...

The tractor beam was too strong. We were now both going up. Up to the ship. Up to the collector. Up to our...

"Why are you whistling?" I asked.

"I'm not whistling!" yelled the Smear. "I'm signaling."

"Signaling who?"

"The mice platoon."

I looked around. The mice were nowhere to be seen. All I could see was the bottom of a spaceship and a future life frozen in an action pose.

I hoped it was a good action pose. You know, something dignified.

We were almost at the ship!

"Try whistling again," I suggested.

The Smear looked up to me. "I can't do it again. Two whistles is an entirely different signal."

"DO IT AGAIN!" I screamed.

"Okay, but you're not going to like it."

The Smear whistled again. And finally, just as we were about to be swallowed up by the ship, the cavalry arrived.

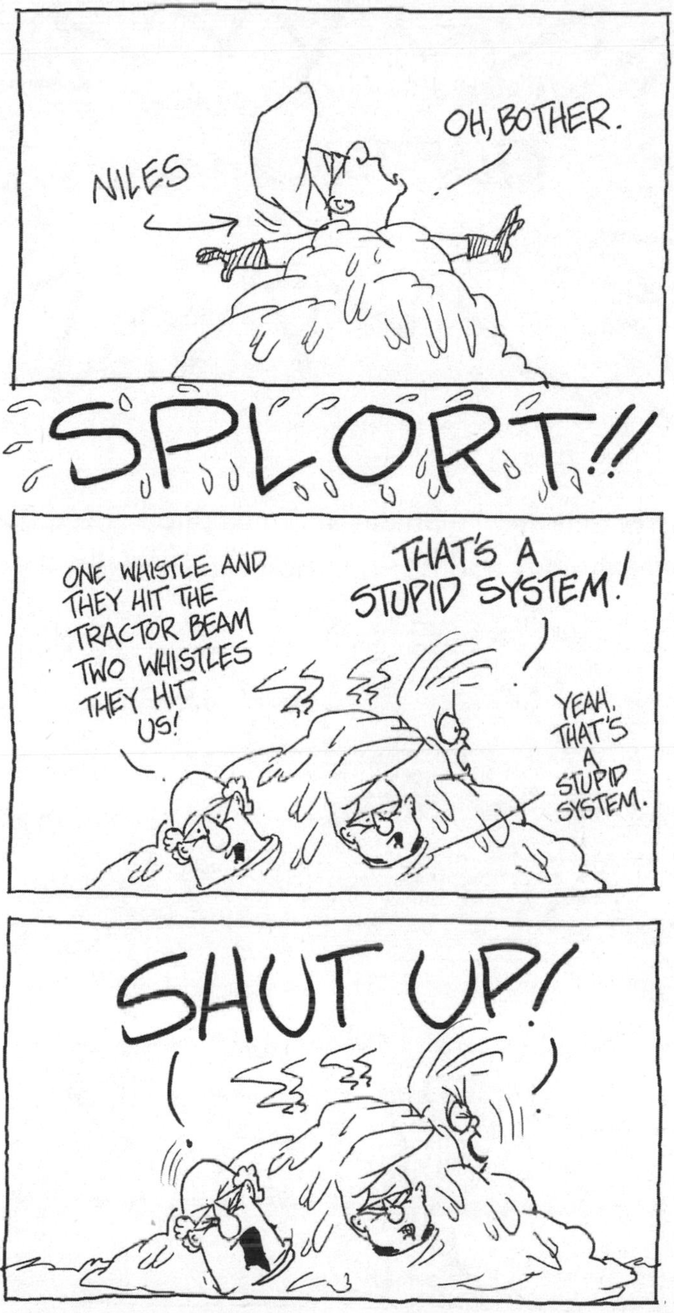
NILES
OH, BOTHER.
SPLORT!!
ONE WHISTLE AND THEY HIT THE TRACTOR BEAM TWO WHISTLES THEY HIT US!
THAT'S A STUPID SYSTEM!
YEAH, THAT'S A STUPID SYSTEM.
SHUT UP!

CHAPTER 15

After making the Smear and me fall on Niles, the mice fired a Grade Z Stain Bomb at the spaceship.

GRADE Z STAIN BOMB

SPLOOSH

MICE

SPLAT!

It didn't do much at first. Then...

"It's eating through the ship!" I cried.

The Smear said, "The stain won't bring it down, but it should scare them away."

And that's exactly what happened.

"What was in that stain?" I asked.

"Ghost peppers and cola," said the Smear. "Eats through most alloys and stomachs in seconds."

"Is it safe to come out now?" asked a voice from the shadows.

"It's safe," said the Smear.

And that's when every kid and lame grownup supervillain and superhero walked into the light.

"They tried to take me?" I asked. "But none of you?"

The Smear smiled. "Like I said, you're special."

Everybody nodded. Except Niles, of course.

He eyed me. "I still think you're a jerk."

"What are we going to do?" asked Octavia.

The Smear smiled. He straightened up to his full height. He sucked in his gut. He cleared his throat. "We're going to do what supers do...

SAVE THE WORLD!

"Was that totally necessary?" I asked.

The Smear glared at me. "You're no fun."

"Fine. So how are we going to save the world?" I asked.

"We're going to work the problem!" barked the Smear. "We're going to put our heads together and figure out who this collector dude is and how to stop him. And most important of all, we're going to keep him from getting you."

I pointed out the obvious. "We're not exactly the A-team here."

Mr. Beet spoke up. "We weren't even worth kidnapping to be frozen in action poses. What makes you think we can save anyone?"

"Are you going to accept the judgment of your worth by some crazy collector?" asked the Smear. "Or are you going to live up to your potential and prove him and everyone else wrong?"

Moldy Dave raised his hand. "Can I exfoliate first?"

Anvil Head raised his hand. "My space plane is in the shop."

Toxic Girl raised her hand. "My cape is at the cleaners."

Bobzilla raised his hand. "I have a dentist appointment."

Javy raised his hand. "I have a Secret Lair midterm I have to study for."

And so on.

I walked over to the Smear.

...WE'RE DOOMED, RIGHT?

SO DOOMED.

CHAPTER 16

Let's recap.

The cool supers have been taken hostage by an evil collector person who likes his action figures life-size (and frozen alive!).

Standing against this crazy collector with a ginormous spaceship (with a small hole in it) are a motley group of lame supers and Junior Super Academy kids.

And mice. Can't forget the mice.

"Maybe he won't come back," said Javy.

"He'll be back," said the Smear.

Me, the Smear, lame supers, and superkids were meeting in the Mighty Mite Memorial Cafetorium.

THE MIGHTY MITE MEMORIAL CAFETORIUM

DEDICATED TO MIGHTY MITE, WHO TRAGICALLY LOST HIS LIFE WHEN HE WAS MISTAKEN FOR A PEPPERCORN AND ACCIDENTALLY GROUND INTO MEAT FOR TACO TUESDAY

"He'll be back," I said. "For me."

"He has everyone else," pointed out the Smear.

"Everyone cool," added Moldy Dave.

Octavia stood up. "Hold on. How do we know the collector is a him? It could be a her. It's just like all superdudes to presume the bad guy is a guy. We girls can be evil, too!"

This is so true.

"Him or her," said the Smear.

"Or it!" said Iron Dude, who was rumored to have alien blood in his family tree.

I said, "I think we should focus on the next step."

"Run?" suggested Moldy Dave.

"No one's running," said the Smear. "We have a duty to rescue our super brothers and sisters."

Worm Boy spoke up. "Mr. Awesome once said I lacked backbone."

"You're part worm," I reminded him.

"I don't think he was making a point of fact," said Worm Boy.

"The Blue Wasp said I lacked subtlety," the Woodchipper remarked.

Anvil Head raised his hand.

The Smear interrupted. "I know. I know. Some cool super said you were hardheaded."

"Mack in the Box said I had a screw loose," corrected Anvil Head. "My head is forged. No screws."

Suddenly, every super in the place had a gripe about the cool supers.

The Smear shouted them all down.

They chilled.

"Look, I get it," said the Smear. "Those guys and girls and things can be jerks. I know. I was banished for twenty years! No one here has to tell me there's a class system at work among the supers. I've lived it. But look where it's gotten them. They're frozen! In uncomfortable positions! They need *our* help! This is our time! This is our moment to shine! Just because they go low, doesn't mean we can't go…"

"HIGH!" screamed the Smear. "We go HIGH!"

The Smear continued. "If we rescue them, then *we're* the heroes. *We're* the cool supers. *They'll owe us.*"

AHHHHHHHHHHHH...

"I think they're starting to get it," I whispered to the Smear.

"Always appeal to greed," he nodded.

Yet another teachable moment with the Smear.

"First step," barked the Smear. "We gather intel. We figure out where that ship is from."

"How?" asked Javy.

"You want to know where an alien ship is from, you ask aliens."

"Bob and Dave!" I cried.

ROCK MONSTERS

BOB

DAVE

"Bob and Stan," said the Smear. "Dave is on vacation. Stan is his twin brother."

ROCK MONSTERS

BOB

STAN

"Where are they?" asked Javy. "Do they have a secret lair? Is it in Norway? I bet it's in Norway. I bet it's an impenetrable fortress of *doom*, hidden in a fjord in Norway. I like saying fjord. Fjord. Fjord. Fjord. Everybody say it with me!"

"Stop talking," said the Smear. "They don't live in Norway. They live in Malibu. A very low-key, tasteful place on the beach. Right next to Tom Hanks."

"Oh!" said Javy. "I like Tom Hanks."

"He's a jerk," said the Smear.

"Nooooooo," Javy moaned.

"So, we're going to Malibu."

"We don't have time," said the Smear. "We can Skype them instead."

The Smear pulled out a laptop. "What's the wi-fi password?"

"Seriously?" said the Smear.

CHAPTER 17

"Stan? Bob? Can you hear me now?" the Smear yelled into his laptop.

Rock monsters Stan and Bob shook their rock heads. Behind them a classic Malibu Beach House Party raged.

"Great. They can't hear me. This is why no one teleconferences," said the Smear.

I said, "No one teleconferences because no one wants the other party to know they're not wearing pants."

"Really?" said the Smear

I nodded. "I know these things."

"It's true!" said Tom Hanks, from the laptop. "I'm not wearing pants!"

"It's working!" I said. "Hey! Tom Hanks!"

"Get off the line, Tom. I'm onto you," said the Smear.

Tom ignored the Smear. "Ain't no party like a Malibu Beach House Party 'cause a Malibu Beach House Party *rocks!*"

"Hose him down," said the Smear. "We've got a situation here."

Someone yanked Tom Hanks off-screen and we were left with Bob and Stan.

TOM IS ALWAYS OVER HERE.

WE THINK HE'S LONELY.

"Whatever," said the Smear as he held up his phone. "We need some help. Do you guys recognize this ship?"

Stan nodded. "That's a ZZ-Class Cephalopod from Nilax-12 in the Plax system."

"Z-Class," corrected Bob.

"Oh. Right," said Stan. "ZZ-Class had an extra lava extractor."

"Lava?" I asked.

"The ship runs on lava," said Bob.

I said, "That seems like a serious safety issue."

"It is," said Stan. "The Z-Class is highly unstable."

"Unsafe at any speed," added Bob.

"What's it doing here?" asked the Smear.

"Probably stolen," said Stan. "The Plax system doesn't allow intergalactic travel due to space pirates smuggling Nilaxian root beer."

"Okay. I'll bite," said the Smear. "What's the deal with Nilaxian Root Beer?"

"Turns your pee purple," said Bob.

"Cool!" chimed Javy.

Stan said, "It also conveys gene-specific super-powers."

"Gene-specific?" I asked.

"It bonds with your DNA to super-strengthen your weakest trait," said Bob.

I said, "So if I'm short, it makes me tall?"

"Or if you lack ambition, it makes you want to...

TAKE OVER THE WORLD!

"I still don't know what the heck anyone does with the world once they take it over," I muttered.

"I've always wondered that myself," said Stan.

"Seems like a lot of work," added Bob.

"Okay," said the Smear. "We have someone in an alien spaceship sucking up supers. What's their next move?"

"They want me," I reminded him.

"Other than that," said the Smear.

"Refuel," said Stan. "It's a long trip back to Nilax-12."

"That means they'll need lava!" I said. "Where's the nearest active volcano?"

Javy raised his hand. "Ooh! Ooh! I know! Spleen Island."

SPLEEN ISLAND

Javy said, "Actually, it looks more like a slug, but Spleen Island is a cooler name."

"Thanks, guys," said the Smear to the screen. "We can take it from here."

"Tom! Put that down! That's our cousin, *not* a doorstop!" yelled Bob, off-screen.

Stan said, "We gotta go."

The screen went blank.

I turned to the Smear. "Take it where?"

"To Spleen Island, of course," said the Smear.

"And then what?" I said.

The Smear said, "We'll find the spaceship, take down this collector person, and rescue your parents and all the supers."

"How?"

"Have you ever jumped off a cliff and made antigravity boots on the way down?"

"Um. No." I said.

"Well, you're going to learn," said the Smear, as he turned to the crowd. "We're all going to learn."

Javy raised his hand.

"How much time before we hit the bottom of that cliff?" I said.

The Smear looked at his shoes. "Not enough."

CHAPTER 18

The lame supers, the superkids, the Smear, and I all piled into Bee Boy's blimp and set off for Spleen Island.

BEE BOY'S BLIMP →

It was going to take a day or so to get there (blimps are slow). Plenty of time to plan Operation

Kick Butt and Take Names (though not enough time to workshop a better name). Also, plenty of time for me to repair my friendship with Octavia.

I found her in the back of the blimp reading *Teen Super.*

"Hey," I said. "Got a second?"

Octavia looked up. "Absolutely."

I said, "I just wanted to—"

"Time's up."

I couldn't be sure, but I think she was still mad at me.

"I just wanted to apologize," I said.

"You should never apologize for who you are," she said.

"I'm a jerk."

"Yes. And you should own it. Like a true supervillain."

"You know I'm not a supervillain."

"You don't know what you are. One second you almost tickle Niles to death. The next second you're too good to fight Niles. And the next second you want to abandon the super life and be a librarian."

"Librarians are superheroes. With their super reading powers, they can become anyone and go anywhere in the universe. They're time-traveling shapeshifters in sensible shoes."

The corner of Octavia's mouth curled up. Just a little.

"I'm not laughing," she said.

I smiled. "And I'm not smiling."

"Whatever."

"Look, I like to read. I like to know stuff. Stuff that might come in handy. Like, did you know that turtles can breathe through their butts? I learned that from a book."

"What book? *Go, Butt-Breathing Turtles, Go?*"

"No. *Make Way for Butt-Breathing Turtles!*"

"You're weird."

"You asked."

Octavia stared at me and shook her head. "Can you at least try to get along with Niles?"

"Why?"

"Because he's not so bad. And because we're all in the same boat...er...blimp. His parents are frozen in that spaceship, too, you know. And...

I sighed. "Okay."

There was a beat of silence. Then I said, "On second thought, maybe it was *Good Night, Turtle Butt-Breathers.*"

Octavia sighed. "Shut up."

We didn't say anything for a bit. Then...

CHAPTER 19

We arrived at Spleen Island. Javy was right. It did look more like a slug.

SLUG-
LIKE

You know, if you add eyes and a mouth.

I approached the Smear on the blimp bridge. He was putting the final touches on his "jump off a cliff and build the antigravity boots on the way down" plan.

He pointed to a map of the island. "We'll launch a small reconnaissance mission here."

"Great, I can't wait," I said.

"You're not going anywhere," said the Smear.

"What?"

"This collector wants to collect you. Once he has you, he'll take off and we'll lose everyone he's captured. Including you."

"But I can help," I protested. "I'm, you know, special."

"We can't risk it. Now I'll team up with Octavia, Niles, and—"

"Niles?"

"Yes, Niles. Along with Moldy Dave, Mr. Beet, and Worm Boy. We'll explore the island, locate the ship, and then figure out what to do next."

"All while I stay here on the blimp and do nothing."

"You won't be doing nothing. You'll be surviving to fight another day."

"But my parents!"

"We're going to get them back. Your job is to

make sure they have someone to come back to."

"A useless son."

"Victor, you can't always be the hero. Some-times you have to be the dude in distress. Some-times you have to let someone else save *you*."

Dude in distress?

HELP?!

The Smear smiled. "You're going to be fine. Your parents are going to be fine. All those cool supers who are frozen in action poses on that alien ship are going to be fine. Just sit tight and let us fight this battle."

With that, the Smear exited the bridge and I was left alone.

Alone with my thoughts.

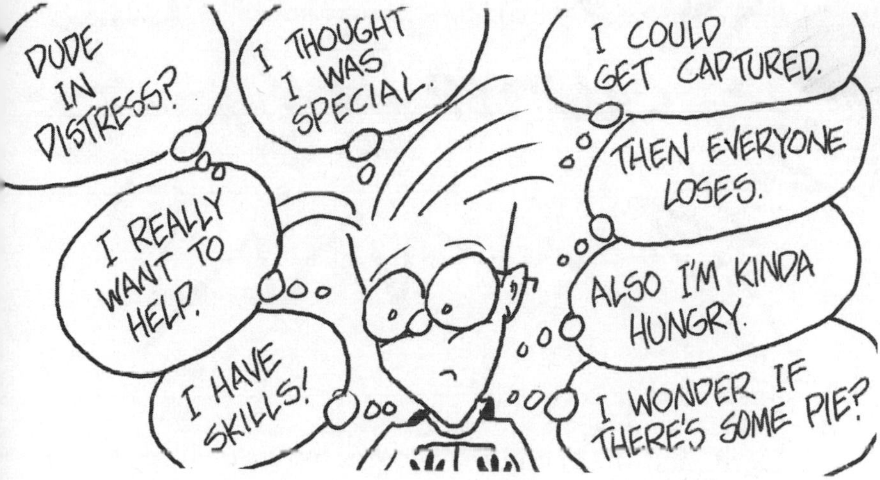
DUDE IN DISTRESS?
I THOUGHT I WAS SPECIAL.
I REALLY WANT TO HELP.
I HAVE SKILLS!
I COULD GET CAPTURED.
THEN EVERYONE LOSES.
ALSO I'M KINDA HUNGRY.
I WONDER IF THERE'S SOME PIE?

I think too much.

CHAPTER 20

I watched the recon team parachute down to the island.

Despite what Octavia said, I really hoped Niles landed in a volcano.

Kidding. Sort of.

Not really.
After they landed, I beat it to the blimp bridge

to follow their progress. We'd wired the team with
GPS sensors to track them on the island.

The group landed on the beach and quickly
headed inland along a small stream.

I was watching the monitor with Dr. Deodorant.

"They have no idea where they're going, do
they?" I said.

Dr. Deodorant said, "If the spaceship is there,
the Smear will find it."

I said, "I wish I had your confidence."

"I've faced off against the Smear plenty of
times. He knows what he's doing."

"We're talking about the Smear, right? Old?
Out of shape? Stains people?"

"Well, my superpower is making things smell nice."

"Yeah. Sorry about that."

"Says the kid who tickles people. You know, it's not the superpower, it's the power of the super."

Right. The power of the super. But what does that mean? Superpowers or not, right that second I felt pretty helpless. Everyone was down on the island doing cool recon stuff and I was stuck on the blimp with my thumb up my nose. Actually, it wasn't up my nose. That's just an expression. I don't actually ever put my thumb up my nose. Just want to make that clear. Never.

Where was I? Oh, right. Helpless.

Dr. Deodorant pointed to the blimp's radar.

I said, "It looks like a storm."

Dr. Deodorant pointed outside. "There's not a cloud in the sky."

We both immediately turned to a window.

"Someone needs to warn them!" I cried.

"Who?" asked Dr. Deodorant.

CHAPTER 21

I landed on the beach and ran toward the stream.
From the beach, I could see the spaceship as it let
loose dozens of robot drone pterodactyls headed
straight toward the island.

The recon group was under the island's jungle canopy. There was no way they could see what was headed their way. They were sitting ducks.

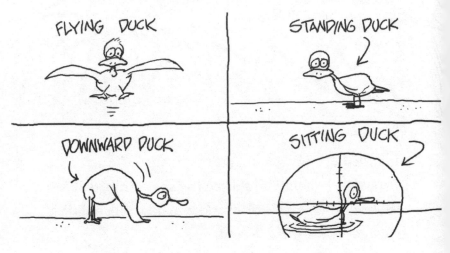

FLYING DUCK

STANDING DUCK

DOWNWARD DUCK

SITTING DUCK

I got to the stream and ran into the jungle. I figured the group was about ten minutes ahead of me.

The second I got off the beach, the heat and humidity hit me. It was like running into an invisible sponge, and the sweat started pouring off me. I slowed my pace, but pushed on.

The stream narrowed. I abandoned the trail and raced up the stream. I turned a bend and ran straight into...

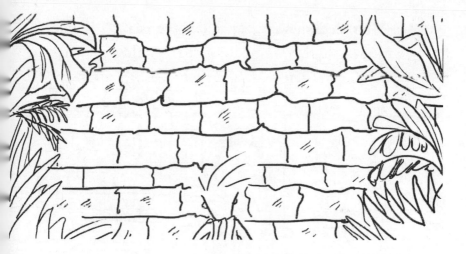

The wall went up about thirty feet and stretched out in both directions. The only way through was up. I started climbing.

I got about halfway when I heard them.

"This seems like a bad idea," said Octavia, on the other side of the wall.

"It's fine," said Niles. "The others are too slow. We can find the ship ourselves."

The others? Too slow? Octavia *and* Niles? Together?

Alone?

I climbed faster.

I got to the top just in time to see Octavia and Niles disappear through a doorway.

Wait. A doorway?

It was an ancient temple. Or maybe a cleverly disguised secret lair. But probably just an ancient temple. They had gone inside what looked like a back entrance.

"Dave, will you hold still!" yelled a familiar voice.

I turned to see Moldy Dave, the Smear, Mr. Beet, and Worm Boy on the far side of the courtyard in front of the temple. I instantly realized why they had fallen behind Octavia and Niles.

In the heat and humidity, Moldy Dave had become mostly mold with very little Dave.

"It itches! It really itches!" cried Moldy Dave.

Worm Boy added, "It doesn't smell too good, either."

The Smear and the other supers were trying to save Moldy Dave from himself. They were clawing and scraping at the moldy sarcophagus that was swallowing him. But just as soon as they removed one chunk, another sprouted in its place.

"This is ridiculous," said the Smear. "We're going to medevac Dave so we can keep moving."

"I can move. I can help!" said Dave, who clearly couldn't do either.

"No, you can't," barked the Smear. "Mr. Beet, get the blimp on the horn. Now where did Octavia and Niles go?"

I pointed. "They went that way."

The Smear looked up. "Victor! What are you doing here?"

"I'm here to warn you!" I yelled.

"About what?"

I pointed, "THEM!"

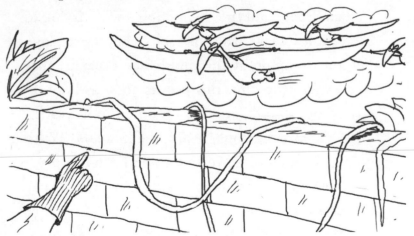

I had a nanosecond to make a decision. Should I risk everyone's safety or just mine?

Easy decision.

Hard to implement.

CHAPTER 22

You might be thinking how selfless of me to sacrifice myself so the others could live.

But you would be wrong.

See, as I was beating it out of there, being trailed by a swarm of robot pterodactyl drones, I noticed that Octavia and Niles had emerged from the temple.

While it was true that I was acting very bravely, it was also true that Octavia and Niles *saw* me acting very bravely. Octavia would have no choice but to admire me, and Niles would melt into a puddle of jealousy and shame.

I mean, no good deed should go unwitnessed, right?

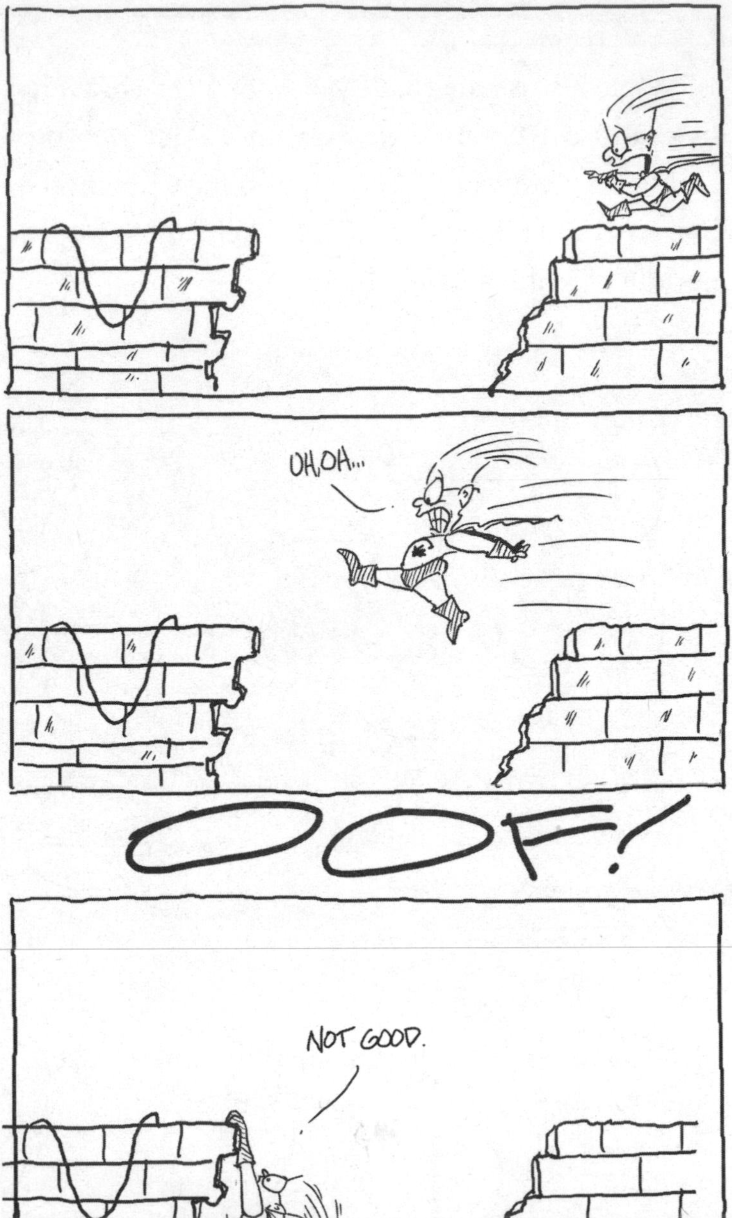
OH,OH...
OOF!
NOT GOOD.

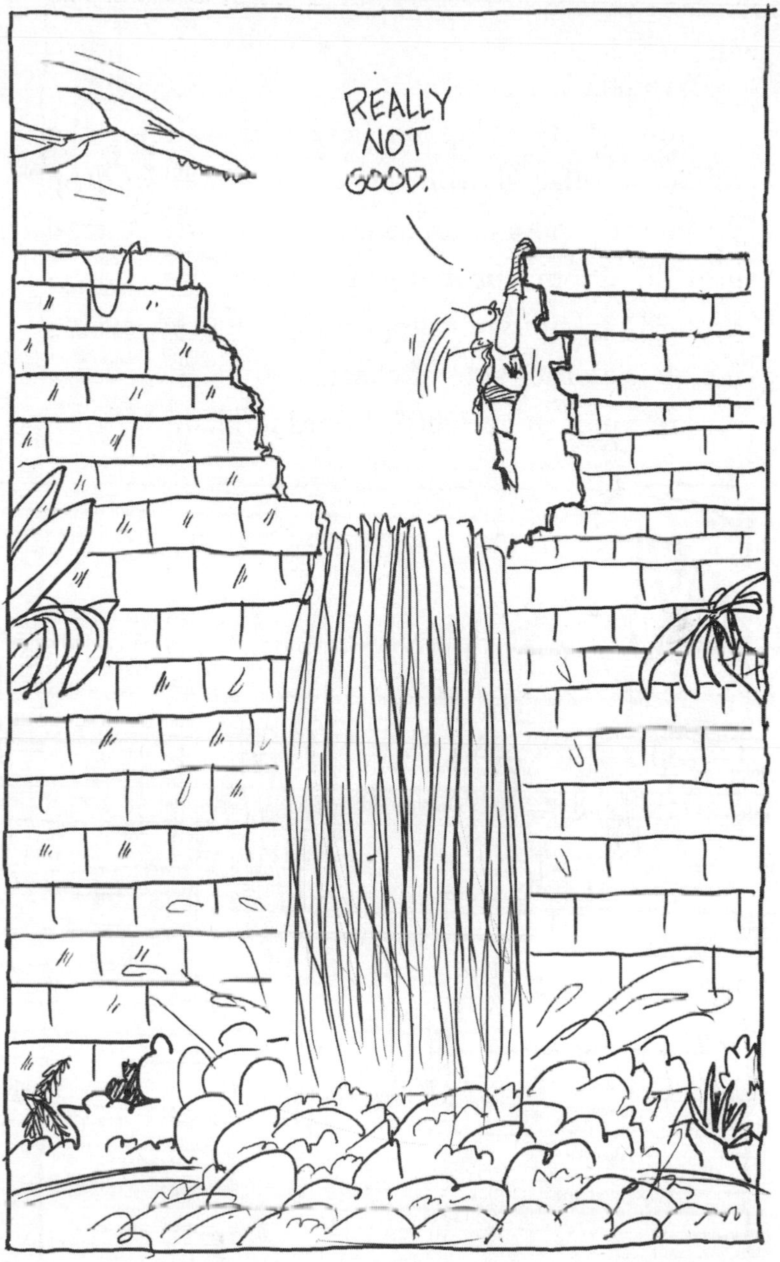
REALLY NOT GOOD.

Wrong.

Now what? Hang on here and wait for the robot pterodactyl drones to capture me? Or drop down into a pool of unknown depth and bacterial growth? Or maybe battle the robot pterodactyl drone that suddenly appeared, hungrily eyeing me on the other side of chasm?

Are robot pterodactyl drones ticklish?

Time to stop, drop, and scream.

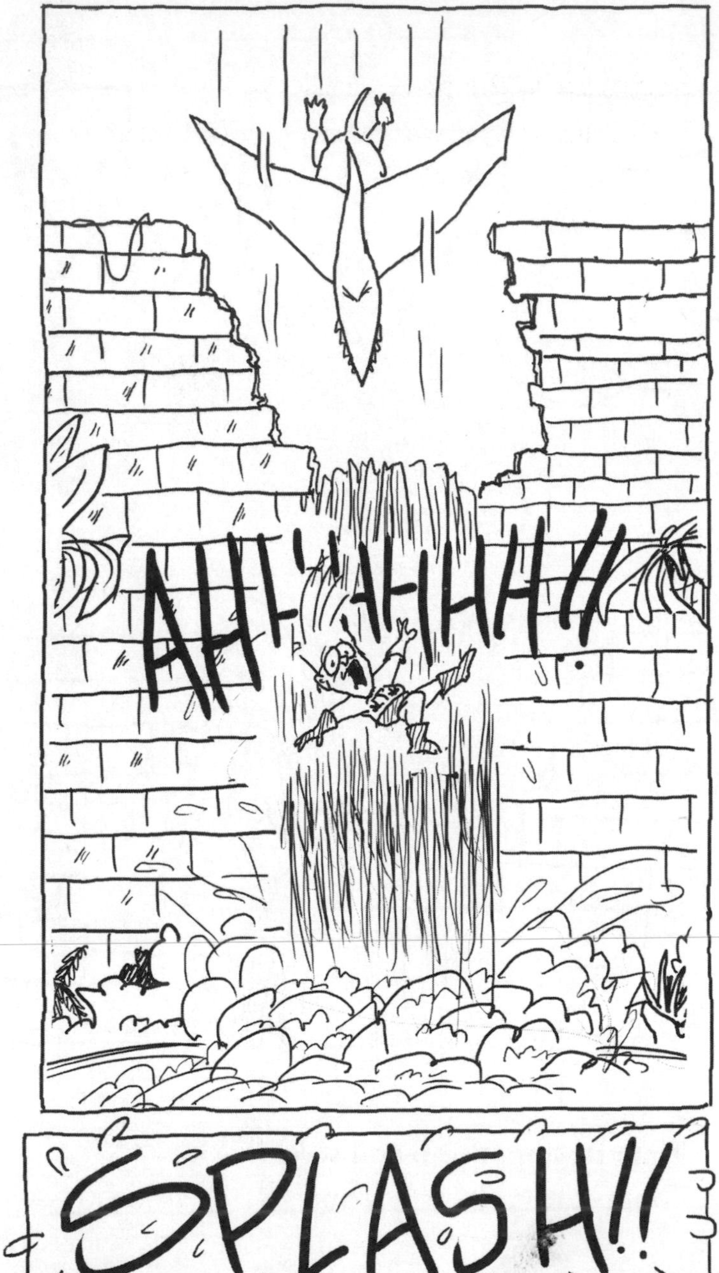
AHHHHHH!!
SPLASH!!

Fortunately, the pool was deep.

Unfortunately, it was stocked with piranhas.

In case anyone asks, sacrificing yourself for others is really, really hard.

Turns out piranhas are ticklish. Who knew?

I bobbed to the surface and started swimming.

I didn't have to go far before I got sucked into the current and was headed straight for the rapids.

I looked back to see I was still quite popular with the locals.

My plan was working. Sort of. I'd succeeded in leading the drones away from the rest of the group. Now I just had to escape myself. But how? That's when I saw my chance straight ahead.

I made it! I was safe! The group was safe! Everyone was safe! Except, you know, for my parents and the frozen supers. But hey, one thing at a time.

As I closed my eyes and floated through the dark cave, I decided that since the recon group was out of danger, I'd let them finish their work while I headed back to the blimp. After all, the collector was still after me and I didn't want to make his job too easy.

"Welcome to Spleen Island," said a woman's voice.

I opened my eyes. I was no longer in a dark cave. I was in an enormous underground submarine port.

I closed my eyes again. "Well, poo."

CHAPTER 23

So I got caught.

Which, as I've explained, should mean that our story is over. The collector person has his kid and can now take off with his other frozen supers for universal parts unknown.

But, as you can clearly see, we're not even close to finishing this story. So, maybe I'm not all that caught. Maybe I'm just *sort of* caught. For now.

Maybe I have a trick up my sleeve.

PROPERTY OF
VICTOR SPOIL
300 DEPLORABLE WAY
MUNCIE, IN

No tricks. Just a name label Mom sewed into the sleeve of my costume.

Rats.

Before I could check my other sleeve, a giant claw plucked me out of the water and deposited me on the deck in front of the Scary Boss Lady and her small army of robot squirrels.

VICTOR SPOIL,
I PRESUME...

"Yeah, so?" I said. "And who are you?"

The Scary Boss Lady in Black said, "Rogi is my name. I am the Commodore's assistant."

"The Commodore?" I asked.

"He's so excited to meet you," said Rogi. "You're the final piece in his collection."

"So I've heard."

"Why so glum? A great adventure awaits!"

"Frozen in an action pose for all eternity?"

"Oh, that. That's just for display purposes. For showing off, you know, at parties. That's not why the Commodore collects supers."

"So why does he collect them?"

"You're a kid. Why did you collect action figures?"

"To play with them. You know, make them take naps, do their homework. Line dancing. That sort of thing."

"Seriously? Most kids fight them."

"I'm not like most kids."

"I can see that," she said, as she turned to the robot squirrels. "Now, seize him!"

The squirrels bound my hands and feet and then started to "escort" me off the dock and through a doorway and into the Commodore's secret lair.

RIGHT THIS WAY...

Rogi continued, "You're going to have so much fun! Not like here on Earth where all your

superbattles are fake. Where we're going, super
battles are very, very real."

"You're taking us hostage to fight?" I asked.

"Hostage? No, no, no. We're liberating you to
pursue your natural destiny. You're supers, not
professional wrestlers. You don't need a script to
fight. All you need is some proper motivation."

"Like saving the universe?" I asked.

"Like saving yourselves!" she chimed.

We continued down a passageway carved out
of the rock. Lit torches illuminated our way. It
was all very textbook "secret lair." Right down
to the safety posters and loudspeaker announce-
ments.

IT HAS BEEN 43 SECONDS SINCE THE LAST ACCIDENT

PEASE BE ADVISED THE MENU IN THE LAIR CAFETERIA HAS CHANGED. THE JELL-O TODAY IS BLUE INSTEAD OF PURPLE. THAT IS ALL.

GROAN!

"Okay, wait," I said. "You're taking us to fight what? Each other? Other supers from other planets? Something else?"

Rogi said, "Yes to all three. But mostly something else."

I didn't want to know. But I had to know.

"Like what?" I asked.

"Like that," she pointed. "And that. And that. And that."

I was pretty sure I could take the hamster (they're quite ticklish), but everything else (including the bunny) scared the snot out of me.

"We're gladiators," I realized. "You're collecting gladiators to fight across the universe."

I said, "And if we die in the process?"

"You'll have died for a good and noble cause," she said.

CHAPTER 24

According to Rogi, the gladiators fight in front of a galactic video audience. Kind of like one of those music competitions on TV...except the loser dies.

After a few more twists and turns in the passageway and another cafeteria menu adjustment (mutton nuggets instead of turkey meat loaf), we finally entered the Commodore's central lair.

SHARK MOAT

At Super Junior Academy, we'd describe this lair as "classical villain." Lots of dials and blinking lights and, of course, a shark tank as the central focus. A more modern take (neoclassical villain) would lose the sharks and replace them with bears.

BEAR MOAT

"Welcome to the Nexus," said Rogi.

"Nice shark tank," I said.

"We like it," she said. "Now if you'll excuse me, the Commodore will be with you shortly."

The robot squirrels tipped me upright and sat me in what looked like a repurposed dentist's chair.

As I waited to meet the Commodore, I got a bit nervous. Not freaking out exactly, but anxious. It wasn't the sharks or the robot squirrels or the mind-reading upside-down spaghetti-strainer thingy. That stuff was par for the supervillain course. What really got the hair to stand up on the back of my knees was the sense of evil calm about the place. Like, this collector dude, whoever he was, did this stuff all the time. Like it's routine to kidnap supers, flash-freeze them, and then whisk them off to galactic parts unknown and make them fight. Against their will. To the death.

No big deal. Just another day in the lair. Ho-hum.

Evil isn't always flashy fireworks and long-winded monologues. Sometimes it's quiet and boring and very, very deadly.

Suddenly the monitors all came on.

Wait. Did that mean the Smear and the others were under surveillance this whole time? Did that mean my sacrifice was a waste of time?

"That's correct," said a deep, sinister voice. "And yes, I'm reading your thoughts. My evil lair is *not* boring, I'll have you know."

I turned to the shark tank. In the center was a holographic projection of a very large head. A very large, scary head, with flaming hair, a permanent snarl, and several acne scars.

HUMMMM

I'M THE COMMODORE!

"Your hair is on fire," I said.

The Commodore said, "I'm aware of that."

"So, you sent the robot pterodactyls after my friends, knowing I would have to come warn them."

"Yes."

"When I did, you went after me, not them."

"You're very special. Those others? Not so much," he cackled.

"I'm not that special."

"Oh, no. You're the *most* special. In fact, you're

a freak among freaks. You're a *good* supervillain!" Very rare. You'll bring in the crowd. In fact, you'll be the main event!"

"What if I don't want to be the main event?"

"Then I'll kill all your friends and blow that blimp out of the sky."

It's not so much that he just threatened to kill all my friends, it's that he did it so casually. Without any sense of what it meant to me. Or anyone. It's the lack of caring that was so terrifying.

"You're...you're bluffing," I said, my voice trembling.

The head turned to one of his robot squirrels typing at a computer. "Brad, fire me up a lava burst across the bow of that blimp."

"Sure, boss," said Brad. He clicked his mouse.

I watched the monitor.

He wasn't bluffing.

"Fine," I said. "Let my friends go and I'll become a gladiator of the galaxy."

"*The* gladiator of the galaxy," he corrected.

Right. *The* gladiator of the galaxy. The good supervillain vs. that bunny that probably shoots lasers out of its butt.

Not sure I'd survive that. Not sure there was a super anywhere on Earth that could.

That's when I felt my stomach fall through the chair. And even if I could make antigravity boots on the way down like the Smear said, they would be useless because, you know, stomachs don't

wear boots. Maybe slippers. Or socks. But definitely not boots.

STOMACH

STOMACH
WEARING A SOCK

Then, just as my stomach was about to hit
bottom and splat into a million gooey stomach
splats, my brain shifted into hyperdrive and I had
an idea. Not a great idea. Not my best idea. But
the best great idea I could come up with when
your stomach is about to go all ka-blooey.

I stared at the burning head. "You have all the
top supers on the planet, right?"

"Every last one."

"Then why am *I* the headliner?"

"What do you mean?"

"I can't shoot acid out of my nose."

The Commodore flinched. "No one can. And why would you? Gross."

"And I can't snap my fingers and stop your heart."

"Is that a thing?"

"And I can't kick your butt so hard that it swaps places with your brain and then everyone calls you butt-brain and you die of shame and, you know, because a butt makes a really terrible brain."

The head rolled its eyes. "Now you're just being silly."

"I'm not. I'm dead serious. There is one super who does all that and more. And you don't have him."

"Who?"

I inspected my fingernails. Then I stopped because they were dirty. The submarine port was really muddy. "Never mind. You don't seem interested."

"I am. I'd really like to know."

"He's probably not available anyway. He's pretty shy. Likes his privacy."

"Tell me who he is!" the Commodore demanded.

I shook my head as much as the spaghetti strainer would let me. "I don't know."

"*Tell me!*"

"Fine. But you didn't hear it from me." I winked.

The flaming head got even flamier. "TELL ME NOW!"

"Ready?"

"Yes!"

"You sure?"

"YES!"

"You're *sure*-sure?"

"Tell me before I feed you to my sharks!"

I grinned. "Okay. His name is...

...CAPTAIN CHAOS!!

CHAPTER 25

"Captain Chaos?" said the Commodore.

"Right," I said. "The greatest super on the planet."

"I never heard of Captain Chaos."

I shrugged. "What a shame."

"You're lying."

"I'm not. You can ask anyone." *Please....Please don't ask anyone.*

The Commodore turned to Brad again. "Brad, get me the *Collector's Guide to Earth Supers.*"

Brad rummaged through some papers and retrieved a thick book.

The Commodore said, "See if Captain Chaos is in there."

The Commodore turned back to me. "You're making him up."

"I'm not," I said. "Like I said, he's very shy. Almost retired. Hardly ever comes out. No fake battling."

"Prove it," barked the Commodore.

Okay, Tickle Boy, now what? My stomach was up in my throat. And those stomach socks were starting to stink. Have I mentioned how my ears sweat when I'm freaking out? It looks like my ears are crying. Crying ears! I'm not making this up. Unlike Captain Chaos, whom I'm totally making up. Hmm...making stuff up...that's it! I have to keep going. I've gotten this far with my imagination, I can't stop now!

"What's wrong with your ears?" asked the burning head.

"Nothing. So, you know as you're coming in from space, there's that landmass? The one that looks like a boot?"

"Italy?"

"Right. Italy. Well, it didn't always look like a boot. It used to look more like a sock or an elbow."

"Well, that boot shape is because of Captain Chaos. He was battling the Spore and took a swing and missed, which carved out that whole boot shape with one punch."

"I'm skeptical," said the Commodore.

I nodded. "Of course. Who wouldn't be? I tell you what, let me get him in here and if he's everything I say he is, you let everyone go and he can be your main event. No one can survive Captain Chaos. Not even that bunny that shoots lasers out of its butt."

"What?"

"Captain Chaos is the real deal."

The Commodore bit his lip. "You're almost certainly lying to save yourself. But..."

This was it. I almost had him. I just had to close the deal.

I leaned forward against the spaghetti strainer and looked the flaming head in its evil eyes. "But what if I'm *not* lying?"

The Commodore didn't say anything for a minute. Then he turned to Brad. "Brad, what do you think?"

Brad said, "We have a week of lava refueling here before we can leave. Maybe we see what the kid's got. Can't hurt."

Have I mentioned how much I like Brad?

"Okay," said the Commodore. "Bring me this Captain Chaos and we'll see. No promises."

"Cool!" I chirped, not feeling cool at all, but more like a kid who just won a game of Go Fish with Death.

"Hold on," said the Commodore. "I've got to make sure you come back. I'll need a hostage."

"You already have my parents!" I cried.

"A new hostage," he insisted. "How about that guy?" He nodded at one of his screens.

Terrific. Another dude in distress. And a dude I don't particularly care for. Not that I wouldn't come back for him. I have to. Or do I?

After all, I'm a supervillain.

But a *good* supervillain.

Do they make halos in black?

CHAPTER 26

I escaped!

Sort of. Not really. The Commodore let me go, but only to retrieve a superhero who doesn't exist. And if I don't return with the nonexistent Captain Chaos, he'll throw Niles into a volcano. Which, of course, I'm not going to let happen.

But a supervillain can dream, can't he?

The robot squirrels and Rogi released me near the beach.

"You have one week," said Rogi.

"I don't know if I can find Captain Chaos in a week," I said.

Rogi stared at me. "One week."

Stupid scary lady assistant. What sort of dumb name was Rogi anyway? Dutch? Icelandic? Des Moinian? Or maybe it's just a made-up name. Or maybe something obvious spelled backward.

Oh.

Rogi and the robot squirrels (not a bad band name) left me on the beach. I could see the blimp

in the distance. I was about to wave it down to get
me when I heard a shout.

The recon group ran toward me. Everyone was
safe. Well, everyone but Niles.

"Victor! What happened?" said the Smear.

"It's a long story," I said.

"They have Niles!" cried Octavia.

I said, "I know."

"You know?" said Octavia.

That's when I told them everything. And a lot
of stuff they didn't know. And a lot of stuff they
didn't want to know.

"Captain Chaos?" whispered Octavia. "There's no such thing as a Captain Chaos! What were you thinking?"

"I don't know," I said. "I thought maybe we could, I don't know, come up with something." I pointed to the Smear. Like you said, build those antigravity boots on the way down?"

The Smear sighed. "Me and my big mouth."

Octavia glared at me. "This is all your fault."

I pointed at the Smear, "He started it!"

The Smear held up his arms. "Let's work the problem, people!"

Worm Boy frowned. "Captain Chaos would have to have the powers of Awesome Man,

Titanica, and SuperZeus combined."

"In other words, the most powerful super in the universe!" added Mr. Beet.

"Can he shoot acid out of his nose?" asked Moldy Dave.

"How did you know?" I said.

"Or *her* nose," corrected Octavia.

"Hold on!" I cried. "She, or he, or it doesn't even have a nose. Because she, or he, or it doesn't even exist!"

"What?" I asked.

The Smear smiled. "I know a gal."

CHAPTER 27

"You know a what?" I said.

"A woman who can help us," said the Smear.

We were back on the blimp. Everyone was gathered on the bridge. The Smear stood in front of a large map.

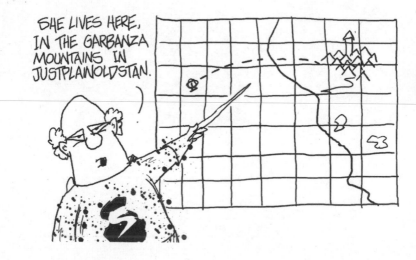

SHE LIVES HERE, IN THE GARBANZA MOUNTAINS IN JUSTPLAINOLDSTAN.

"Justplainoldstan? My nana is from Justplain-oldstan!" shouted Javy. "She always said it smelled like old socks and cheese."

"Can we focus here?" asked the Smear.

"So what's in Justplainoldstan?" I asked.

"The greatest robot maker in the world," said the Smear.

I said, "I don't think a robot is going to fool this guy. He seemed pretty sharp. I mean, for a burning head."

"She makes the best robots. You know Professor Perilous?" asked the Smear.

"Sure. Everyone knows Professor Perilous," said Javy.

PROFESSOR PERILOUS →

SHOOTS GHOST PEPPERS* OUT OF HIS HAT ←

QUITE LIFELIKE →

*SUPER SPICY

"Are you saying..." I started. "Wait. No."

"Yes. He's a robot and Madge made him."

I paused. "He does have that eye tic thing."

"And his hat was always randomly exploding," added Javy.

"Nobody's perfect," said the Smear.

"This robot maker. Her name's Madge?" asked Octavia.

MADGE FREDENSTEIN

The Smear said, "Great-great-great-great-grandniece of the famous Dr. Victor Frankenstein. Six times removed. Changed the name to, you know, avoid all the negative baggage."

Octavia said, "Yeah. The whole 'reanimating

dead people and then not being able to control your creation' thing."

"That's why Madge only does robots. A lot easier to turn off," said the Smear.

I'm used to weird stuff. I'm a super, after all. But this was off-the-charts bonkers. How on earth could the great-grandniece of Dr. Frankenstein make the most powerful super robot in the universe in a week? And...

"Why would she help us?" I asked.

"She and I go way back," said the Smear.

"Please don't tell me you used to date," I said.

"Okay, I won't tell you," said the Smear.

I said, "The last time I heard about you dating someone, we ended up being attacked with a tuba. Is there anyone we need to save the universe that you *haven't* dated?"

"Back in the day, I was a player," said the Smear. "You know, before the banishment and the weight gain."

"Great. You're saying the success of this whole thing rests on this Madge not being able to resist your charms?"

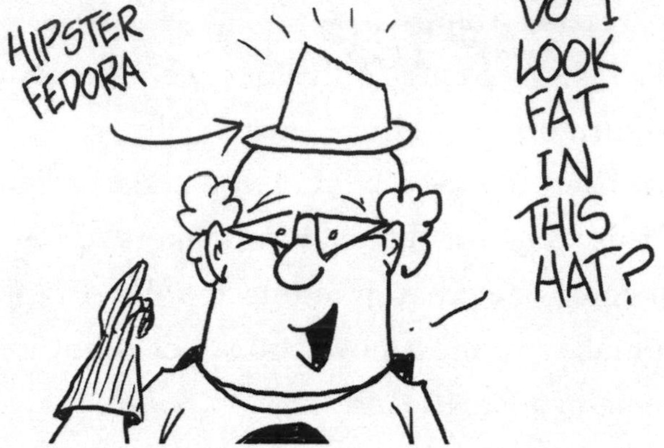
HIPSTER FEDORA
DO I LOOK FAT IN THIS HAT?

I did not answer.

CHAPTER 28

A blimp isn't the fastest mode of transportation. It was going to take a couple of days to get from Spleen Island to the Garbanza Mountains, where Madge lived. Plenty of time to reflect, catch up on my reading, and continuously apologize to my friend who happens to be a girl.

"He's going to be fine," I said. "Even if Captain Chaos doesn't work out, I'll go back, turn myself in, and take his place."

"And then you'll be a prisoner and end up fighting some giant alien sloth that spits acid," said Octavia. "That's just as bad."

"I'm confused," I said. "You're mad at me now for getting Niles captured *and* you'll be mad at me later when I turn myself in for him and fight giant alien acid-spitting sloths?"

Octavia stared at me. "Yes."

"I can't win."

"No, you can't."

"You did notice that I sacrificed myself back there on the island to the robot pterodactyls so you and others could be safe?" I pointed out.

"I did," she said. "I also noticed that you noticed that I noticed."

"There's nothing wrong with noticing someone is noticing."

"But noticing someone is noticing is not the same thing as *not* noticing someone is noticing."

"So, it would have been better if I had sacrificed myself and not noticed you were noticing."

"Yes. Because then you're not sure anyone is noticing, but you do it anyway because you don't care if anyone notices."

"But I *do* care!"

"I noticed."

Octavia has a lot of rules. She should write them down.

OCTAVIA'S RULES

1. DON'T GET NILES TAKEN HOSTAGE.
2. DON'T SWAP PLACES AND GET YOURSELF MELTED BY ACID-SPITTING ALIEN SLOTHS.
3. DON'T TRY TO GET NOTICED FOR DOING WHAT YOU SHOULD BE DOING ANYWAY.
4. FIX ALL OF THIS WITHOUT GETTING HURT.
5. I RESERVE THE RIGHT TO CHANGE THESE RULES AT ANY TIME.

"I have a headache," I said.

Octavia smiled. "I'm not surprised."

Javy entered our cabin. "Hey, we're almost to the robot lady's mountain laboratory."

I said, "Something tells me it's just a house on a big hill with a lot of rusting cars and old toasters in the yard."

Javy looked at Octavia. "What's wrong with him?"

Octavia stood up to leave. "He's got a headache."

After she was gone, I said to Javy, "She's mad at me."

"I know," said Javy. "I read her mind."

"I thought you had to put your hands on people or something."

"Not always. Sometimes I just need to be near them."

"That's super creepy."

"I can't help it. It's my superpower."

I sighed. "Well?"

"Well what?" asked Javy.

"What is she thinking?"

"Oh. She's worried."

"About me?"

"Yes. I mean, I think so. I mean, it's either you or her parents or whether we're going to have fish sticks again tonight."

"Fish sticks? I thought you read minds!"

"I do. But remember? I have dyslexia!"

I groaned.

"I do know one thing for sure," said Javy. "You don't have to be a mind reader to see she cares about you."

CHAPTER 29

After my failed attempt to strangle Javy, I went to
my blimp bunk. I lay down and stared at the ceiling. There was a lot to think about. My parents.
The alien collector dude. Captain Chaos. Octavia. Life. Death.

Fish sticks.

I was having second thoughts. Well, actually
they're third thoughts. Maybe fourth. It's hard to
keep track.

I asked the ceiling, "Why me?" Per usual, the
ceiling didn't respond.

Stupid ceiling.

"Why so low, Joe?"

I looked over at the doorway. It was the Smear.
"My name is Victor," I said.

"Victor doesn't rhyme with low."

"It rhymes with loser."

"No, I'm pretty sure it doesn't."

"It does if I say it does!" I yelled.

"Okay. Sure," said the Smear. "But you're not a loser."

"Let me count the ways," I said.

"Okay. I agree, there have been a few set-backs," said the Smear.

"A few?"

"This isn't all your fault, you know. You didn't ask that alien collector dude to kidnap your parents."

"No. But why do I have to be the one to fix everything? I'm just a kid!"

"You're a special kid."

"*Stop* saying that!"

"It's true."

"No, it isn't. I'm just a kid who'd rather be reading books than saving the world."

"Victor, what's going on?"

"Nothing. Everything. I don't know."

"What are you afraid of?"

The Smear sat on my bunk. He put his hand on my shoulder. "You're not going to fail."

"You don't know that."

"If you try—if you do your best—then you can never fail."

"If I try and I don't get my parents back. Or Octavia's parents. Or the rest of the supers. And they end up fighting for their lives. Or if I get captured and end up fighting for *my* life, *I've failed!*"

"No. You'd be dead. There's a difference."

"There's no difference!" I cried.

"Relax. You're not going to die. I won't allow it."

"What do you mean *you?*"

"Listen. I can see you're scared. You'd be crazy not to be."

"I'm *not* scared. I'm *terrified!*"

"No, it isn't," I sniffled.

"Maybe. Maybe not. I don't know. What I do know is that the universe tilts ever so slightly toward good."

"Really?"

"I'm a supervillain. I've lost enough fake and real battles to know that the deck is stacked against us."

"I thought you said good and evil were two sides of the same coin."

"They are. But if you flip that coin a thousand times it's going to come up good five hundred and one times."

"That's not much of an advantage."

"It's just enough advantage. Especially if the flipper is someone like you."

"Me? Why?"

"First, by choosing to make a difference. Second, by actually doing something to make that difference happen. Third, by...by...I forgot what number three was."

"By being me?"

"Well, you can't be me. That would involve a lot of weight gain and avoiding dairy."

"It's not fair."

"It's never fair. But it is interesting. And in the end, if we win, there'll be pie."

"I like pie."

The Smear smiled, "I've heard."

Suddenly the door burst open. It was Javy.

He shoved his phone in my face. "Have you seen this?"

I said, "I saw this poster on the island. I thought it was just pretend. Like something that might happen if I fail."

"It's not pretend," cried Javy. "No fake battles, no scripts—this is all very real. Your parents, my

parents, Octavia's parents…they're all in danger."
He stared at me. "I can read your mind and either
you're craving peanut butter or you understand
what's at stake."

I wasn't craving peanut butter. I knew what
was at stake. I had to save my parents. Everyone's
parents. I didn't have a choice.

I turned to the Smear. "Do you have a coin?"

The Smear reached into his pocket and handed
me a penny.

"Heads is good. Tails is evil," I said.

I flipped.

CHAPTER 30

I was absolutely right about Madge's place.

Not that it made me feel any better.

All of us—the Smear, me, Octavia, Javy, and all the lame supers—gathered at her front gate.

"How do we get in?" asked Javy

I pointed. "There's an intercom."

The Smear walked up and punched the intercom button. "Hello?"

No answer.

"Try again," I said.

"Hello?" said the Smear.

"Madge? Is that you?" asked the Smear.

"Go away! I don't want any!" said the speaker.

The Smear said, "Madge, it's me, Pooky."

"*Pooky?*" I said.

"POOKY?" screamed the speaker.

The Smear smiled. "She remembers me."

"You miserable, low-life, cracker-headed, sop-bellied, pig-butted..."

"...sorry excuse for a super!" growled Madge. "If you don't get off my property in the next three seconds, I will personally come down there and rearrange your face into a relief map of Texas!"

"That was very specific," I noted.

"She's kidding," said the Smear. "She likes to kid."

"Three…two…one!" counted Madge.

"I don't think she's kidding," said Javy.

"You can read her mind?" I asked.

"I'm not going anywhere near her mind," he said.

Then, with a wild creak, the front gates opened.

"See?" said the Smear. "She was kidding."

It will be no surprise to anyone what happened next.

ROBOT VAMPIRES, ROBOT MUMMIES, …AND ROBOT ZOMBIES

"Your relationships never end well, do they?" I asked.

The Smear shook his head. "I've just never met the right girl."

Then, from high on the hill, Madge screamed...

I think the following battle will be best accompanied with awesome sound effects.

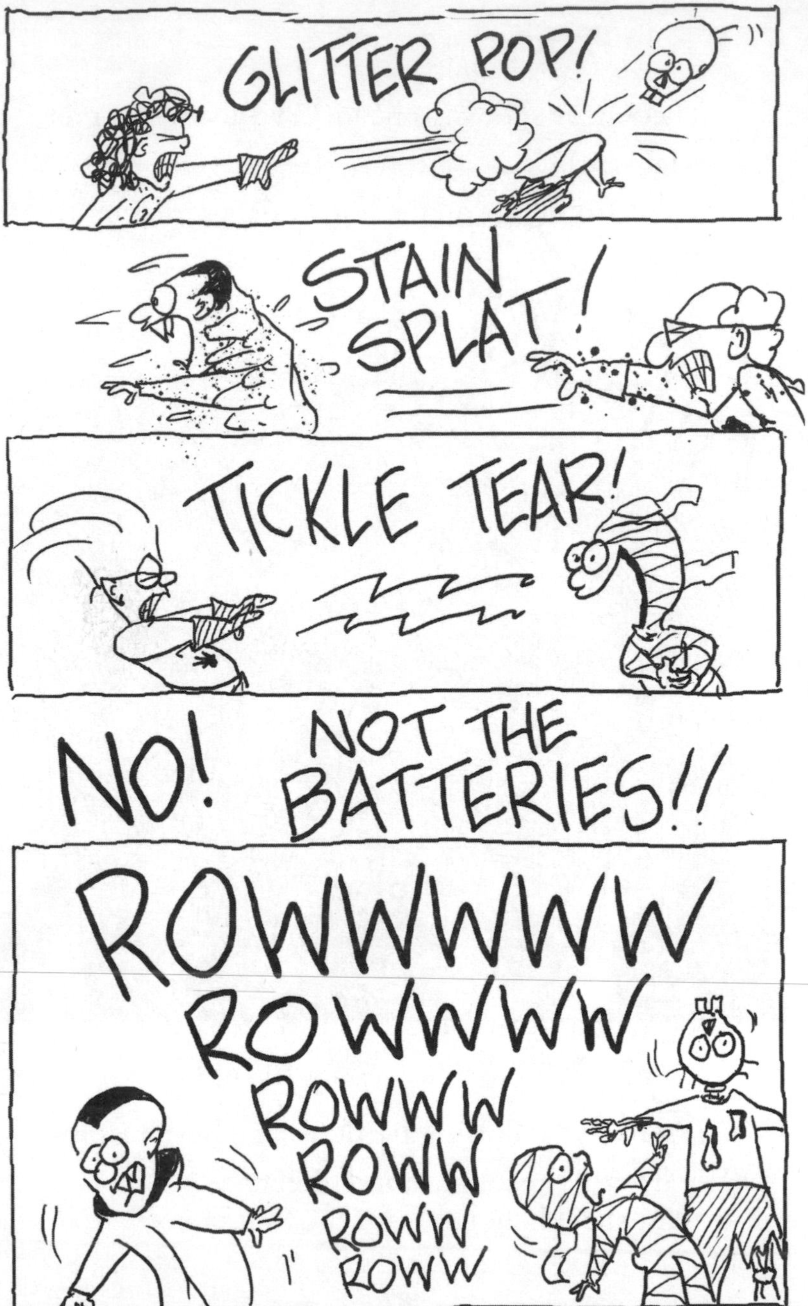
GLITTER POP!
STAIN SPLAT!
TICKLE TEAR!
NO! NOT THE BATTERIES!!
ROWWWWW
ROWWWW
ROWWW
ROWW
ROWW
ROWW

Javy cried, "We won! We won? Wait. How did we win?"

"What do I keep saying?" asked the Smear.

We all recited in bored unison (while rolling our eyes), "It's not the superpower, it's the power of the super."

"And don't you forget it!" barked the Smear.

We all turned and looked up the hill.

"Now that we've destroyed her robot ghoul army, do you think she'll still help us?" I asked.

"Oh, she'll help us," said the Smear.

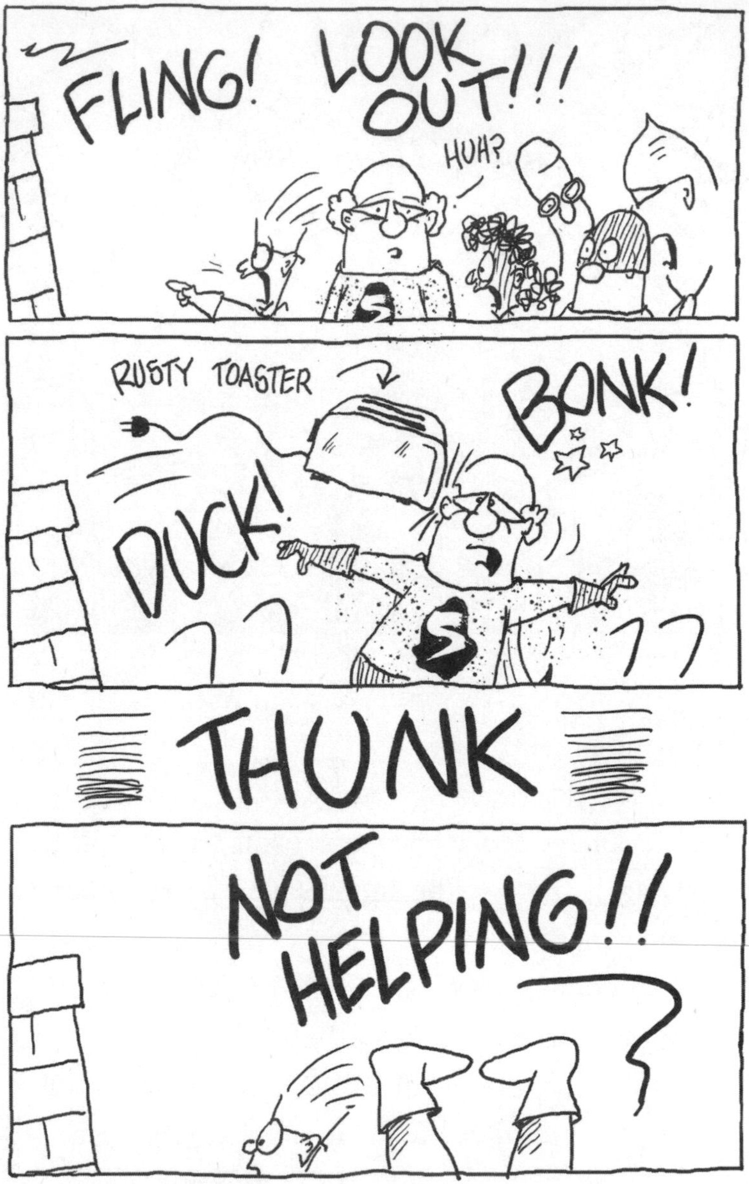
FLING!
LOOK OUT!!!
HUH?
RUSTY TOASTER
BONK!
DUCK!
THUNK
NOT HELPING!!

CHAPTER 31

"I hate you!" growled Madge.

The Smear smiled. "That's been well established."

We had climbed the hill and entered Madge's compound...er...laboratory...er...double-wide robot emporium.

SCRAM!

ROBOT CHIHUAHUA

"We need your help, Madge," said the Smear.

Madge's eyes narrowed. "We were together for three years. Then you just disappeared! No calls. No e-mails. No pictures of those cute cats in sombreros you used to text me…"

MEOW-O

"…NOTHING!"

Javy leaned into me. "I love cats in sombreros."

"Not now," I whispered.

"I should explain," said the Smear. "I was in Australia battling Mighty Moose. He whacked me upside the head with his super horns. I passed out. When I woke up, I didn't know where I was. I didn't know *who* I was!"

"It took months to get my memory back," explained the Smear. "But by then I knew it was too late. You'd never believe me. You'd never take me back."

"You were right!" said Madge.

The Smear got down on one knee. "But I never stopped caring about you. And now I need your help."

There was a moment—a slight beat of hesitation from Madge—and then she turned her back on the Smear. "Why would I ever help you?"

"To save the universe?" suggested the Smear.

"What did the universe ever do for me?" said Madge.

The Smear looked around the yard. "Good point."

Madge folded her arms. "I wouldn't help you if you were being drowned in a vat of seven-layer dip made with low-fat mayonnaise and spray cheese," she sniffed.

Again, that was super specific. And tasty. And not getting us any closer to building Captain Chaos and rescuing the supers.

"Madge, please!" said the Smear. "We're desperate! We need you to build the greatest robot ever invented. Only you can build Captain Chaos."

"Captain Who?" asked Madge. "Not that it matters."

"Captain Chaos," I explained. "A robot super with superpowers that exceed any superhero or -villain. He has to look totally human and we need him in three days."

Madge nodded at the Smear, and my hopes soared. "You're right, only I could do it, but...I won't."

So much for my great Captain Chaos idea.

"As a matter of fact..." Madge went on,

"Javy!" I yelled. "What are you doing?"

Javy said. "It's okay. I read her mind. All she wanted was a hug."

"Ah," said Octavia.

Madge let go of Javy and stepped back. "He's right. I've been alone for so long. I did want a hug."

I rolled my eyes. "That is so lame."

I stepped back. "Whoa. Message received."

Madge looked at Javy. "I will help *you*." Then she turned to the Smear. "*You* can go soak your head in maraschino cherry juice until you rot."

Once again, *so* specific.

CHAPTER 32

Day one: Madge went right to work building the greatest robot super ever. She only had three days, so she had to work fast. She started with a basic skeletal shape.

Then she added a propulsion system.

Next was a flying mechanism.

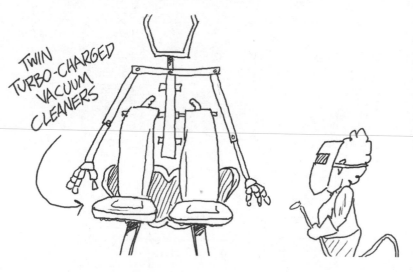

After that, she added the superpowers.

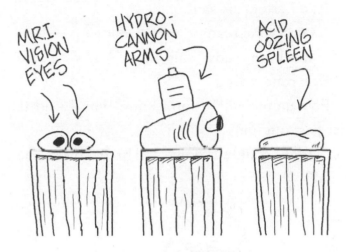

And, finally, she dipped the whole thing in a plastic bath, then encased it in a mold.

"Is this going to work?" I asked the Smear.

"It'd better," he said.

"Is everyone ready?" asked Madge.

"I was born ready," said Javy. "And with a tail."

Everyone stared.

Javy mumbled, "I don't know why I said that last part out loud."

Madge counted down, "Three...two...one... voilà!"

"It looks familiar," I noted.

"Really, like who?" said the Smear.

"You," I said. "You know, except a lot bigger. With hair. And muscles. And without the pot-belly."

"Don't be ridiculous," said Madge. "It doesn't look anything like him!"

CHAPTER 33

Day two: Captain Chaos was ready for the testing phase. We couldn't take him to the Commodore until we were sure he actually did what we said he did.

The first (and most important) test was the Turing Test. The Turing Test is named after the famous computer scientist Alan Turing.

ALAN TURING

COMPUTER SCIENTIST →

MATHEMATICIAN →

CRYPTANALYST (CODE BREAKER) →

PHILOSOPHER ←

BEST QUOTE: "SOMETIMES IT IS THE PEOPLE NO ONE IMAGINES ANYTHING OF WHO DO THE THINGS NO ONE CAN IMAGINE."

1912 – 1954

The Turing Test is a test of a machine's (or robot's) ability to exhibit intelligent behavior equivalent to, or indistinguishable from, that of a human.

And how do I know all this cool stuff about Alan Turing? Hey, I read it in a book. Useful stuff in books. You should try it sometime. I mean, after you finish this one.

So, to sum up, Captain Chaos had to act human enough to make the Commodore believe it; otherwise, we were all going to end up in a volcano.

Madge said, "Victor, do you want to take him out for a conversational spin?"

"Okay," I said, as I looked Captain Chaos up and down. "So what's your name?"

"I am Captain Chaos," he said in a not-too-robotic monotone.

"Where do you come from?" I asked.

"Detroit."

Everyone chuckled.

I continued, "What was it like growing up in Detroit?"

"Cold. Then hot. Then cold again."

Well, he was certainly able to be just as annoying as a human.

"Mr. Chaos, what do you want to do more than anything else?"

"To stop answering stupid questions."

More laughter. Great. A robot comedian.

"Do you know who I am?" I asked.

He said, "You're the kid who asks stupid questions."

"You know, not all humans are sarcastic."

BUT ALL ROBOTS PRETENDING TO BE HUMAN ARE.

Okay. I gave in. He seemed human. In fact, he seemed like a real human jerk.

Next was the superpowers test.
Captain Chaos could fly.

He had MRI vision. That's like X-ray vision but with a lot more detail.

Of course, he could shoot lasers out of his eyes *and* his butt, just like Little Bunny Boom-Boom.

And, you know, the usual: superstrength, superspeed, super-invisibility, supermagnetism, supersmell, superhearing, supertaste, supertouch, and, for some reason, super-yoga-ness.

"I think he's ready," said Madge.
"What's his weakness?" I asked.

She frowned. "He's perfect. He doesn't have one."

"No," I said. "All supers have a weakness. We have to have a weakness or else we'd just always win. And we can't always win. Always winning is boring. 'The super conquered the universe, the end' is *not* a good story. 'The super *tried* to conquer the universe, but tripped over his cape and fell down a bottomless pit of vampire iguanas' is a *great* story."

Javy leaned in, "How'd he get out of the pit?"

I pointed to Javy. "See! Now you've got an audience!"

Madge shook her head, "He doesn't have a—"

"I like pie," said Captain Chaos.

"That's not exactly a weakness," I said. "And besides, you're a robot. You can't eat pie."

He said, "No. I like pie. I *really* like pie."

Madge said, "Okay. Okay. It's a fail-safe. To control him. If we need him to stop or shut down, we use pie."

I smiled. "Just like—"

I looked for the Smear. He was nowhere to be found.

I said, "Where is the Smear? Shouldn't he be here?"

"He's preparing for the trip back to Spleen Island. He's up to speed on all this," said Madge.

Captain Chaos said again, "I really, *really* like pie."

"Yeah, I got it," I said. "I have one last test."

"What now?" said Madge.

I said, "Mr. Chaos, we built you to take the place of all the supers the Commodore captured. You'll be going with him to travel the galaxy and fight other supers and aliens. You may never return. In fact, you may not survive. Are you prepared for that? Are you prepared to sacrifice yourself for us?"

WILL THERE BE PIE IN SPACE?

I DON'T KNOW.

Captain Chaos thought about that for a few seconds. "I serve at the pleasure of the supers."

Get this robot some pie!

CHAPTER 34

Day three: "Is this going to work?" I asked.

"It has to work," said the Smear. "There's no Plan B."

We were back in the blimp on our way to Spleen Island. The Smear and I were in the blimp's hold, plugging in Captain Chaos. He was turned off while his battery recharged.

HE LOOKS REAL ENOUGH.

HE LOOKS EXACTLY AS REAL AS HE NEEDS TO BE.

"You know," I said. "Why don't we just make robots of all the supers?"

"What?" said the Smear.

I said, "Then we wouldn't have to fight in any battles. Real or fake."

"Who would control the robots?" said the Smear.

"We would."

"From a safe distance? Protected from danger? Surrounded by pic?"

"Sure."

"Victor, we each have to fight our own battles. No one can do it for us."

"Wait. Isn't that exactly what we're hoping Captain Chaos will do for us?"

The Smear looked away. "It's different."

"How?" I asked.

The Smear got up to leave. "It just is."

"What kind of an answer is—"

But he was gone. And I was alone. Alone with Captain Chaos. Kind of a clunky name I thought. How about Sam? Or Ned? Or maybe Howard.

HELLO, HOWARD.

Nothing. No response.

Maybe it was a bad idea to name something that you were about to give away.

Or throw away.

I turned to leave.

CREEEAK

I turned back around. Captain Chaos looked

the same. Or did he? Was there just a slight up-
turn to his robot lips? Was he smiling? Or smirk-
ing?

Nah.

I'M
SEEING
THINGS.

CHAPTER 35

On the last day of our deadline, we finally arrived back at Spleen Island.

IT REALLY DOES LOOK LIKE A SLUG.

SPLEEN ISLAND

It was just going to be Captain Chaos, the Smear, and I going down to the island. But the Commodore had other plans.

The Smear was angry. "We brought you what you wanted. You don't need everybody."

Brad moved his pterodactyl's razor-sharp beak next to the blimp.

I looked at the Smear. "Why did we come in a blimp again?"

"Anvil Head's space plane was in the shop, remember?" said the Smear.

"It was due for a fifteen-million-mile tune-up," explained Anvil Head.

"Of course," I said as I turned to the Smear. But he was gone.

But before I could locate him, the blimp landed on the beach. Everyone except the Smear got off.

I turned to Octavia. "The Smear is missing."

"That's weird," said Octavia. "Where would he go?"

"Something isn't right," I said. "He should be here. I can't do this by myself."

Octavia grabbed my arm. "Look around you...

YOU'RE NOT ALONE, VICTOR.

WORM BOY

MOLDY DAVE

MR. BEET

ANVIL HEAD

Sigh. This group? I've never felt more alone in my life.

We started to make our way to the Commodore's secret underground submarine base. It was

tough going. Especially, once again, for Moldy
Dave.

MOLDING
DAVE

The trail stopped at the base of a sheer cliff.
There was nowhere to go but straight up.

Or through.

WELCOME BACK.
PLEASE WIPE YOUR
FEET...

...AND EVERYTHING ELSE.

We entered the mountain. It was a tight fit for Captain Chaos. He had to make accommodations.

After a few minutes, we entered the command center. Suddenly the door behind us slammed shut, separating me, Captain Chaos, and Octavia from the others.

"They'll be fine," said Rogi. "Not everyone needs to see the Commodore."

"Speaking of which, where is the burning head?" I asked Rogi.

"Burning head?" asked Octavia.

"Yeah. He's just a head. On fire." I said. "No body. Just a big, fat, burning head."

Rogi frowned. "The Commodore does *not* have a fat head!"

I said, "Sure. Whatever."

Rogi glared at me. "He's busy planning the battle between the Spoil Sports and the Sparklers."

"Wait," said Octavia. "Our parents are fighting to the death?"

"I was going to tell you," I said.

Octavia cried. "When were you going to tell me? When they were dead?"

"No one's going to die," I said. "The Commodore's going to trade them for Captain Chaos."

Octavia stared at me. I didn't need Javy to know what she was thinking: *I hope you're right. I pray you're right. Because if you're wrong, I'm going to glitter you so hard you'll cry glitter out your ears for the rest of your life.*

I turned to Captain Chaos. Was he still on board with all this?

"The Commodore will be with you shortly," said Rogi as she walked off.

It was the Commodore. His giant head flashed to life above the central console.

I pushed our robot to center stage. "Say hello to Captain Chaos."

Suddenly, a monitor behind the Commodore's head switched on.

It was Niles, suspended above the lava-filled volcano.

Then another monitor flashed.

This one showed my parents and Octavia's parents, squaring off for battle. To the death.

The Commodore smiled. "Impress me."

CHAPTER 36

"Hey, you were just holding Niles hostage till I came back," I said.

The Commodore smiled. "I lied. But don't worry. He'll be fine if everything you say about Captain Chaos here is true. I just find that supers perform much better under pressure."

The Smear gone. Niles hanging over a volcano. Moms and dads battling each other. Octavia staring daggers into me. This can't be happening!

Captain Chaos stepped forward. "You're absolutcly right. I perform much better under pressure.

"Good," said the Commodore. "Let's see what you can do."

With that, Captain Chaos put on a show to

top all shows. He flew. He eye-lasered. He butt-lasered. He MRI'd. He went invisible. He went magnetic. He showed superstrength, superhearing, supertaste, and supertouch. And even topped his yoga move with an even *more* bendy one.

OUCH...

"Very impressive," acknowledged the Commodore. "I especially like the bendy stuff."

"Thank you," said Captain Chaos. "So we have a deal?"

The Commodore shook his head. "No. Unfortunately we do not."

"*No?*" I cried.

"NO!" Octavia shouted, even louder.

"No," said the Commodore calmly. "I have multiple supers frozen in storage who can do every one of the things Captain Chaos can do."

"All in one super?" I asked.

"No. But I don't need a one-man-super-band. I put on battles all over the galaxy and need lots of supers, not just one," said the Commodore. "As impressive as Mr. Chaos is, he's not nearly as valuable to me as you are, Mr. Spoil. You have a history. You defeated Dr. Deplorable with *tickling!* Aliens will pay—and pay well—to see you perform."

I couldn't believe it.

It was over. We created the most amazing super ever and it wasn't enough. I failed. I failed my parents. I failed Niles.

AHHHHHHHH!

I failed myself.

I couldn't watch anymore. Because of me, our parents and Niles were going to die.

CHAPTER 37

"Wait," said Captain Chaos. "I have one more superpower you need to see."

"What?" I said. "That was it. That was everything."

Captain Chaos shook his head. "I saved one power just in case."

What could it be? He already has every superpower there is. Something with mind rays? Radiation? Does he transform into a Dodge Dart?

Nope. It was none of those things. It was the last thing you'd think of, but the first thing that matters in the supers vs. aliens GWBA (Galaxy-Wide Battling Association).

The superpower of entertainment.

WALKA-WALKA-WALKA

POP
LOCK
POP
LOCK
POP
LOCK
POP
LOCK
POP

GRAND JETÉ

"Wow," said Octavia.

"*Super* wow," I echoed.

The Commodore nodded. "Yes. Wow."

There was a long pause while the Commodore furrowed his holographic brow.

That's when I had a terrible thought. This fathead could just take Captain Chaos, me, and the other supers and dump everyone else in the volcano. He already lied about Niles. What's to stop him from reneging on our deal?

"You're going to take me and let everyone else go," Captain Chaos declared.

"Why would I do that?" said the Commodore. "When I can take you, Mr. Spoil, and all the other supers with the press of a button?"

He turned and nodded to Brad the robot squirrel, who had his finger poised above the Launch button. That's when I realized we weren't in a command center. We were on his ship!

"You're not going to do that," said Captain Chaos.

"Why not?" said the Commodore.

"If you do that, I'll do *this*," said Captain Chaos.

RIP!

Uh-oh. Captain Chaos wasn't just a robot, he was a bomb!

"You're bluffing," said the Commodore.

"Try me," said Captain Chaos.

"You won't just be blowing yourself up. You'll be blowing *everyone* up," the Commodore pointed out.

"That's not going to happen," said Captain Chaos. "Because you have a business to run, and you can't do that if you're dead."

"He has a point," I said.

The Commodore looked over at Brad. Brad shrugged. The Commodore turned back to us.

AGREED.

GOOD ANSWER.

CHAPTER 38

We won!

We didn't get blown up.

The Commodore let everyone go and then took off with Captain Chaos.

ZIP!

Did I mention we didn't get blown up?

"Victor!" yelled Mom and Dad.

"You're okay?" I asked.

"Well, your father was frozen into his least favorite action pose," said Mom.

They were fine. I was fine. Everyone was fine.

Except for Niles, that is.

"Hey," I said. "I came back for you!"
"For me? Or your parents?" said Niles.

"That's not fair," I said.

"That's what I thought."

"C'mon, Niles," I said. "Everyone is safe now."

"I've said it before. All you care about is yourself," Niles sneered. "If you'd just given yourself up in the first place, we would all have been released a long time ago."

"You don't know that," I protested. "He could have kept all of us! I did the best I could."

"Your best was Captain Chaos?"

"It worked, didn't it?"

"What. Ever," said Niles as he stalked off.

Octavia watched him go. "You know he was hanging over a volcano for a week."

"And now he's not!" I pointed out.

"Give him time," she said.

Correct me if I'm wrong, but Captain Chaos was my idea. I made him up. I made him up to rescue *everyone*. And rescue myself. I mean, rescue myself after everyone else was rescued. Or maybe while everyone else was rescued? Or maybe before.

Could it be...was I...just rescuing *myself*?

Niles had me all confused. The Smear could straighten this out. Where was he?

I asked Javy, "Have you seen the Smear?"

"No," he said. "But look, it's my parents!"

I couldn't see anything.

"Smell!" he said.

I took a whiff. Ah, Max body spray: tangerine and lava. His invisible parents were back. Good for him.

But what about the Smear?

I looked everywhere, but he was nowhere to be found. No one had seen him since the blimp. That's when it hit me.

The Turing Test. That bit about how we needed to fight our own battles. The fact that when Captain Chaos was talking, the Smear never seemed to be around. Captain Chaos is a robot. He could be controlled externally.

Or *internally*.

The Smear was Captain Chaos!

And now Captain Chaos was gone. Forever.

The Smear had sacrificed himself. He sacrificed himself for everyone. He sacrificed himself for...

CHAPTER 39

"What's the matter?" asked Octavia.

"He's gone," I said.

"Who?"

"The Smear."

"What?"

I explained.

THE SMEAR! CAPTAIN CHAOS! SMEAR INSIDE CAPTAIN CHAOS! SACRIFICE! MY FAULT! SORRY, SO SORRY!

"No!" cried Octavia.

I started crying. Quietly at first, then full-on sobbing.

"He's a real superhero," said Octavia. "I mean, for a supervillain."

I sniffed. "I know what you mean."

We just sat there for a while, not saying anything.

"It's not your fault," said Octavia. "He chose to do what he did."

"I'm never going to see him again."

"You don't know that."

"He's going to die out there fighting that giant hamster."

"What hamster?"

"Trust me. It's huge."

Octavia looked at me. "There is no way the Smear is going to lose to a giant hamster. Maybe a zombie guinea pig. Or, you know, some sort of mutant vampire ferret. But never a giant hamster."

I tried not to smile. But sometimes the more you try not to do something, the more that something happens anyway.

My parents walked up.

"Are you okay?" asked my mom.

Dad asked, "What's going on?"

Octavia explained.

My dad said, "I'm sorry about the Smear, son. He is a great super. Greater than any villain or hero. He's just...

"What is that?" asked Octavia. She pointed at the sky.

I looked up. There was a dot in the sky.

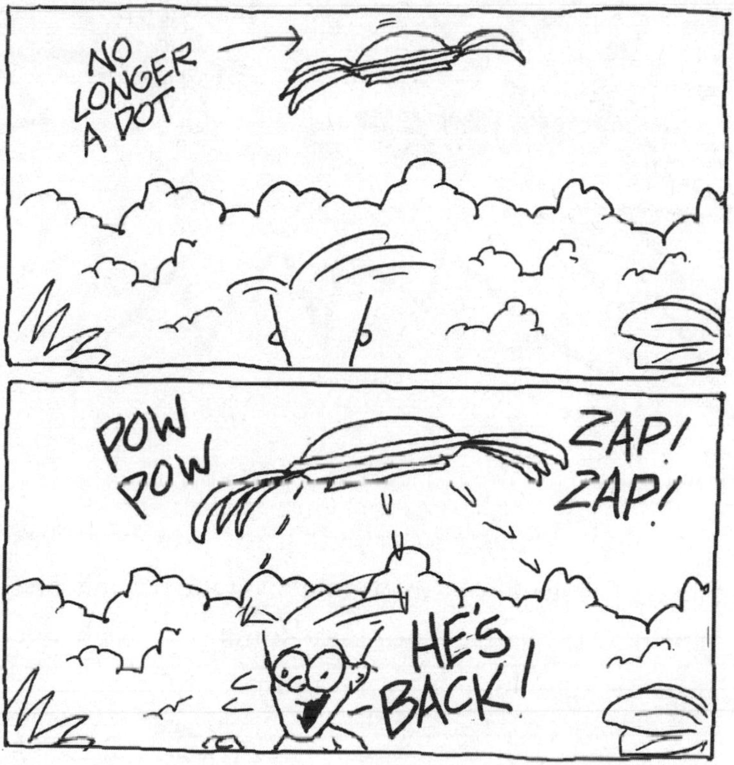
NO LONGER A DOT
POW POW
ZAP! ZAP!
HE'S BACK!

CHAPTER 40

"RUN!"

I don't know who yelled "Run!" Maybe it was me. Maybe it was everyone. Maybe we all just felt it at the same time. Like some sort of cosmic psychic thunderbolt to the brain.

ZAP! ZAP!

But run where?

We were on an island. The only way off was a blimp. A slow, sitting-duck, easy-to-destroy blimp.

I stopped running.

"What are you doing?" screamed Octavia, as she sped past.

As the ship roared by, I blasted it with all the tickling power I had. Which did absolutely nothing to the ship, but everything for everyone else.

One by the one the other supers, both cool and lame, started fighting back alongside me.

Some with more success than others.

Thanks to Moldy Dave's extreme moldiness, the spaceship lost control and crashed into the jungle.

"Three cheers for Moldy Dave!" I cried.

Note to self: we need to work on our cheering.

"I read the Commodore's mind as he sped past!" yelled Javy.

"Seriously? You can do that?" I asked.

Javy said, "It was just for a second. He's angry. He feels ripped off. He wants *you*."

"He must have found the Smear inside Captain Chaos," I said.

Javy looked puzzled. "Why was the Smear inside Captain Chaos?"

"The Smear was controlling Captain Chaos from the inside," I explained. "The Commodore must have discovered him and that's why he came back."

"I should have picked up on that," said Javy.

"You're doing your best," I said. "The important thing is that he was trying to save us."

Javy pointed, "Well, he's not trying to save us now!"

I turned to look.

"That can't be the Smear," I yelled as I dove to safety.

"I can't tell," said Javy. "This always happens when I get nervous. Or embarrassed. Or anxious. Or basically wake up in the morning."

Captain Chaos roared, "Remember when I

said it's not the superpower, it's the power of the super…?"

KA-BLAM

"…I lied."

Hold on. Only the Smear would know that. But it can't be the Smear inside. He wouldn't—

"Smear, it's me!" I cried.

"You're nothing, Spoil," roared Captain Chaos. "And you'll never be anything worthwhile, not even a lame librarian! The only thing you're good for is to put on a show for bored aliens who want to see a fight!"

What's going on? Is the Smear really inside Captain Chaos? If he is, why is he saying all that stuff? It's not true. Unless…

IT IS?

CHAPTER 41

"Now, come with me," said Captain Chaos. "Or everyone else gets the butt-laser. No one wants to see that happen." He started to squat.

It was me or everyone else. I didn't have a choice.

"No, Victor!" called my parents, while Octavia grabbed my arm to keep me from going.

I knew what I had to do. With a heavy sigh, I took a step toward Captain Chaos.

He gave me an unsmiling wink. "Don't worry. We have plenty of pie."

I stopped.

Pie? What's with the pie? He had just been laying into me. Telling me I was worthless...and now he's talking about pie? What's going on?

Pie? *Pie?* What did Madge tell me? That Captain Chaos's weakness was...*pie!*

That's when I remembered something I read.

"SOMETIMES IT'S THE PEOPLE NO ONE IMAGINES ANYTHING OF WHO DO THINGS NO ONE CAN IMAGINE."
—ALAN TURING

Do things no one can imagine.

No one can imagine.

Captain Chaos took a powerful swipe at me. I dove out of the way and landed in some gloppy mud on the side of the trail. I was filthy! Mud everywhere. On my shoes. On my pants. On my best shirt. In my hair. And my hands. I had *just* used sanitizer, too. Now they were covered with mud.

Wait.

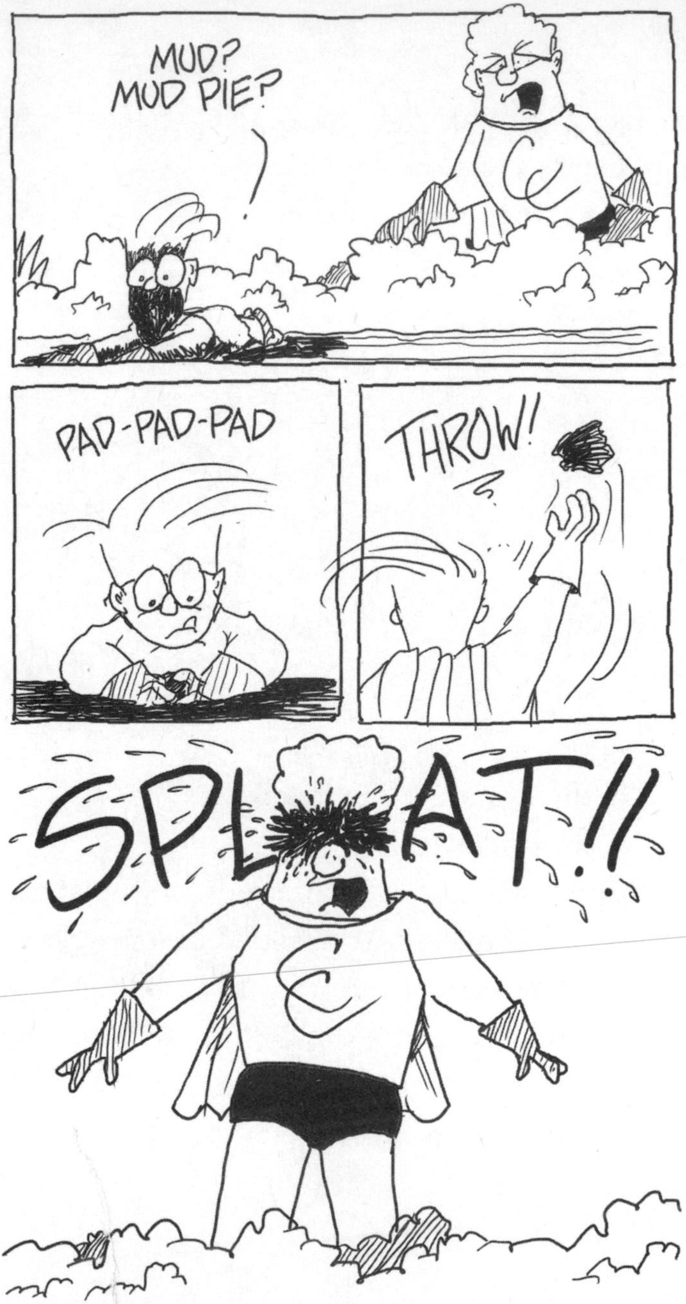
MUD?
MUD PIE?
PAD-PAD-PAD
THROW!
SPLAT!!

Did it work? Captain Chaos just stood there for a second.

Then...

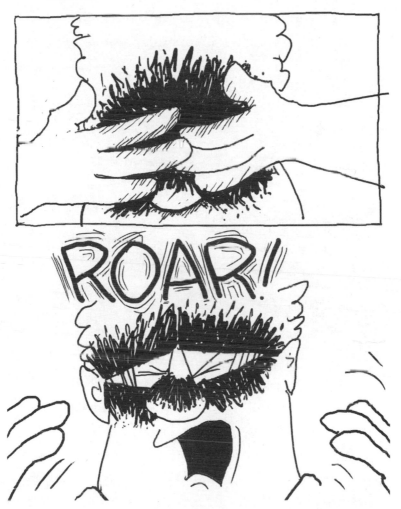

Of course, it didn't work. What was I thinking? It wasn't real pie! And now he's really angry.

"Everybody *run!*" I cried.

I ran. But nobody else did. Octavia yelled something I couldn't hear and pointed back at Captain Chaos. I turned and saw.

The mud must have gotten into his visual circuitry. He was blind! When he tried to wipe away the mud, I shouted, "HIT HIM AGAIN!"

My parents and friends all rushed to scoop up mud and pat it into pies. With whoops and hollers, they let the pies fly.

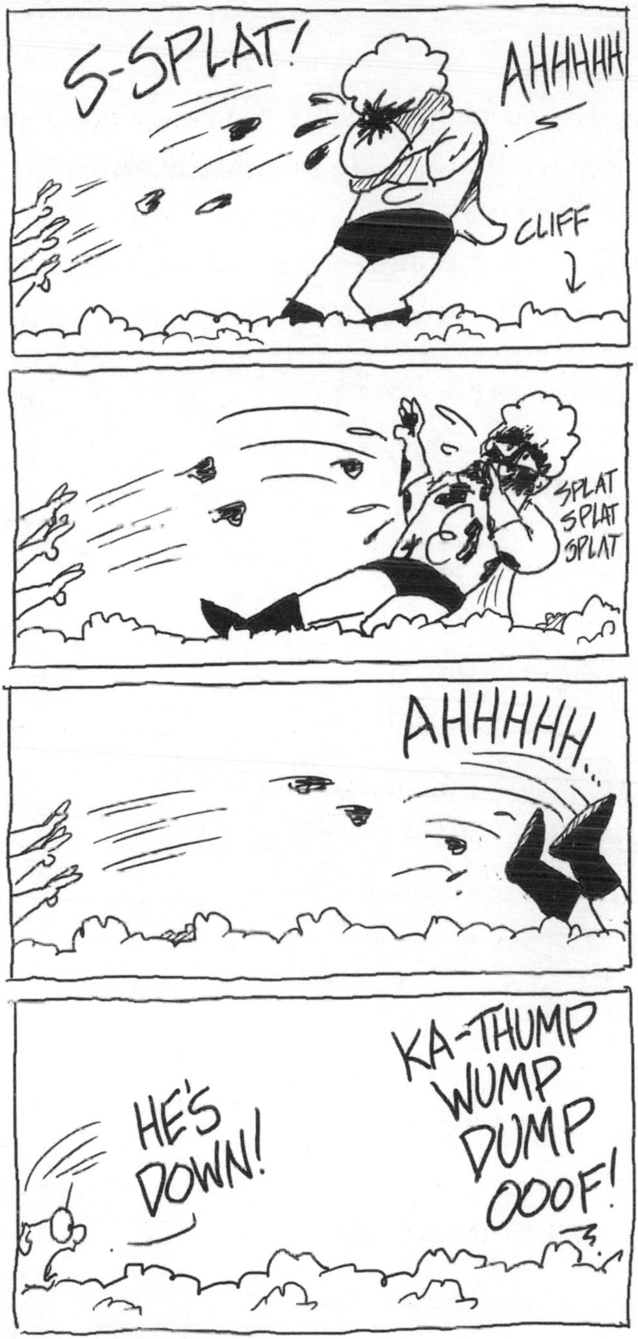
S-SPLAT!
AHHHHH
CLIFF
SPLAT
SPLAT
SPLAT
AHHHHH...
HE'S DOWN!
KA-THUMP
WUMP
DUMP
OOOF!

I peeked over the cliff. Captain Chaos was lying at the bottom. He wasn't moving. I started to go down to rescue the Smear, when out of nowhere, the spaceship—cleaned of all mold—came and vacuumed up Captain Chaos.

As we watched the spaceship fly off, we heard a huge roar behind us. I turned around. Behind me, a space RV landed.

"We got a distress call," said Bob. "It said to make a rescue on Spleen Island, so we jumped in our space bus and got here as fast as we could."

"You're just a little too late," I said.

"Victor saved us himself," said Octavia.

"Well, I had a little help."

I turned to Bob, "I wonder who called you? It wasn't me."

"Or me," said Octavia.

Javy held up his phone. "I got no bars."

All the other supers shook their heads.

That's when Octavia sidled up to me and whispered.

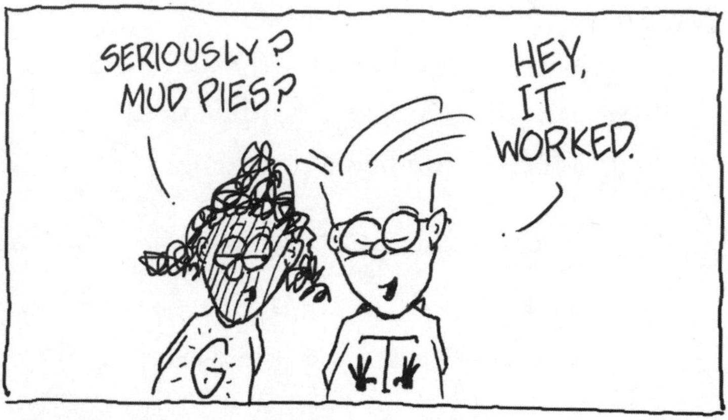
SERIOUSLY?
MUD PIES?
HEY,
IT
WORKED.

CHAPTER 42

Okay. That was a lot to unpack. The Smear saved us, then came back to destroy us and take me with him to fight death battles with giant hamsters. Then, at the last second, I rescued everyone with imagination and pie.

We were all safe on the space bus. Javy, Octavia, and I sat in the back. Niles lurked nearby.

"Maybe he was trying to send us a message," I said, thinking aloud.

"He likes pie and everybody dies?" said Octavia.

I shook my head. "He wasn't going to kill me."

"Lucky you," said Niles from a few seats ahead.

I said, "Look, I'm sorry you almost got thrown into a volcano. I don't know what else to say. I'm doing my best."

"Well, it's not good enough," said Niles, sulking.

Octavia leaned over. "He'll settle down. The volcano singed his eyebrows off. It's a lot to take in."

"They'll grow back," I offered.

"Not helping!" yelled Niles.

Bob and Stan's space bus was very nice. You know, as space buses go.

We weren't all on the space bus. Just me, Octavia, Javy, Niles, our parents, and Stan and Bob,
the rock monsters. The rest of the supers had ar-
ranged their own transportation off Spleen Island.

"Still want to be a librarian?" asked Dad.

"More and more every day," I said.

Dad turned to Mom. "He's still kidding. To
annoy us. It's a supervillain thing."

"I'm not kidding," I said. "This super life
stinks! You almost died. I almost died. I almost
had to battle giant alien hamsters to the death.
The Smear is gone and maybe turned evil. Real
evil, not fake evil. Civilians don't deal with any
of this. Civilians eat cereal and go to bed at nine

thirty. Civilians never, ever shoot lasers out of their butts!"

CIVILIANS ROCK!

"Civilians don't get to ride on space buses," pointed out my mom.

"With satellite TV and Xbox," added Dad.

Octavia's mom said, "Civilians look terrible in spandex."

"Civilians have no idea how to kick butt," said Octavia's dad.

"Or take names," said Javy. "Although, what do you do with names after you take them? Is there a person? A place? And once they're on the list what happens? Banishment? Strapped to rocket and sent into space? Seems harsh."

"Stop talking," I said.

Octavia looked at me. "Civilians never ever get to save the world."

CIVILIANS AREN'T SPECIAL.

They meant well. But the truth is, I didn't feel special. I felt guilty. Captain Chaos was my idea. Without Captain Chaos, the Smear wouldn't have had to sacrifice himself and then go rogue and turn evil and try to kill everyone and then tell us he likes pie and...

Wait. Pie. We need to get some *real* pie!

"Stop this bus!" I cried. "We've got to get pie!"

Everyone stared at me.

"Seriously," I said. "We need pie to stop Captain Chaos if he comes after us again."

Niles said, "I hate pie."

Gee. Big surprise.

Mom turned to my dad. "Is he still trying to irritate us?"

"Yes," said Dad. "And I couldn't be prouder."

Can you divorce your parents? Is that a thing? Maybe it should be.

CHAPTER 43

It took a bit of badgering, but we did stop for pie.

When we re-boarded the space bus, I explained why I thought the Smear was really trying to help us.

"He's just pretending to fight us," I said. "He probably got caught by the Commodore inside Captain Chaos. When the Smear tried to say he was always against us, the Commodore told him to prove it. So, the Smear had to pretend to destroy us in order to save us."

Octavia asked, "And the pie?"

"It's Captain Chaos's weakness. His fail-safe," I explained.

Octavia shook her head. "You know that makes no sense."

"It will," I said. "Trust me. It will."

My mom said, "It was simpler in my day. We got up. We kicked butts. Butts got kicked. We went to bed. Then we did it all over again the next day."

"Nowadays, it's so complicated," said Dad. "There's good guys who are bad guys and bad guys who are good guys and bad guys pretending to be worse guys but who are really still good guys. It all just gives me a headache."

I shook my head. "It's not complicated. It's simple! The Smear is a good guy. He's always been a good guy. Even when he's pretending to be a bad guy!"

I thought about doing a flow chart...

Then I thought better of it.

I finally said, "Like I said, just trust me."

Octavia smiled. "We do."

"You do?" I said.

Niles said, "I don't."

"Ignore him," said Octavia. "He doesn't see what the rest of us see."

"Is there something stuck between my teeth?" I said.

That's when Octavia turned her afterburner

glare on me. "Sit down. Stop talking. And listen."

Octavia can be very persuasive.

CHAPTER 44

"You can't help it," said Octavia.

"Help what?" I asked.

"You can't help being good. You try to be bad. Well, not bad...more annoying. With all the librarian talk and 'why me' and 'I don't want to be special' stuff."

"But I don't..."

"Stop it! You *are* special. And it's not the tickling. Or the irritating. Or the whining. It's what's inside. It's what's in your heart. You can't help but do the right thing! It's like you were *born to be good!*"

Mom leaned over to Dad. "Should we be insulted?"

Dad said, "I'm not sure."

"At every turn, you've done the right thing," said Octavia.

"If I'm so good, then why is the Smear gone? Captain Chaos was my idea," I said.

"You're not responsible for everyone's choices. You can only do what you can do. So far, that's turned out pretty well."

"Except for my eyebrows," said Niles.

Octavia walked up to my mom and grabbed her purse. She pulled an eyebrow pencil out and went up to Niles.

I looked at Octavia. I looked at my parents. I looked at Javy. I looked at Niles (the eyebrows

really did look nice). I looked at my shoes. I
looked out the window.

Niles lay on the floor of the space bus. He looked up at me. "You saved my life. Why?"

I shrugged. "Like Octavia said, I was born to be good."

CHAPTER 45

"Dagnabit!" yelled Stan from the cockpit. We were almost there!

"Evasive maneuvers!" cried Bob.

As the space bus went into a steep dive, Niles and I rolled down the aisle toward the front.

Meanwhile, more robot pterodactyls pierced the bus from all sides!

Stan yelled, "She's getting unstable!"

Bob pointed. "Look! That arch there. If we can just…"

"I'm right with you!" cried Stan.

I poked my head up and looked out the cockpit.

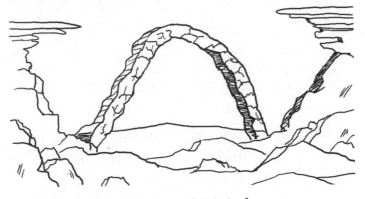

"You're not going to…" I cried.

"GET DOWN!" cried Stan.

I turned to look back down the aisle. We were completely hemmed in.

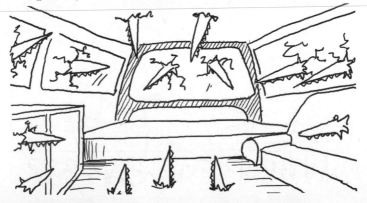

Octavia grabbed me. "I don't want to die."

I hugged her tight. "Me either."

Javy grabbed me. "Or me."

"Is there room for me?" asked Niles. I grudgingly let him hug my elbow.

"Hang on!" yelled Bob.

We hung on. Any second. Any second. Any...

WHAP-BAP-BAP-BAP-BAP

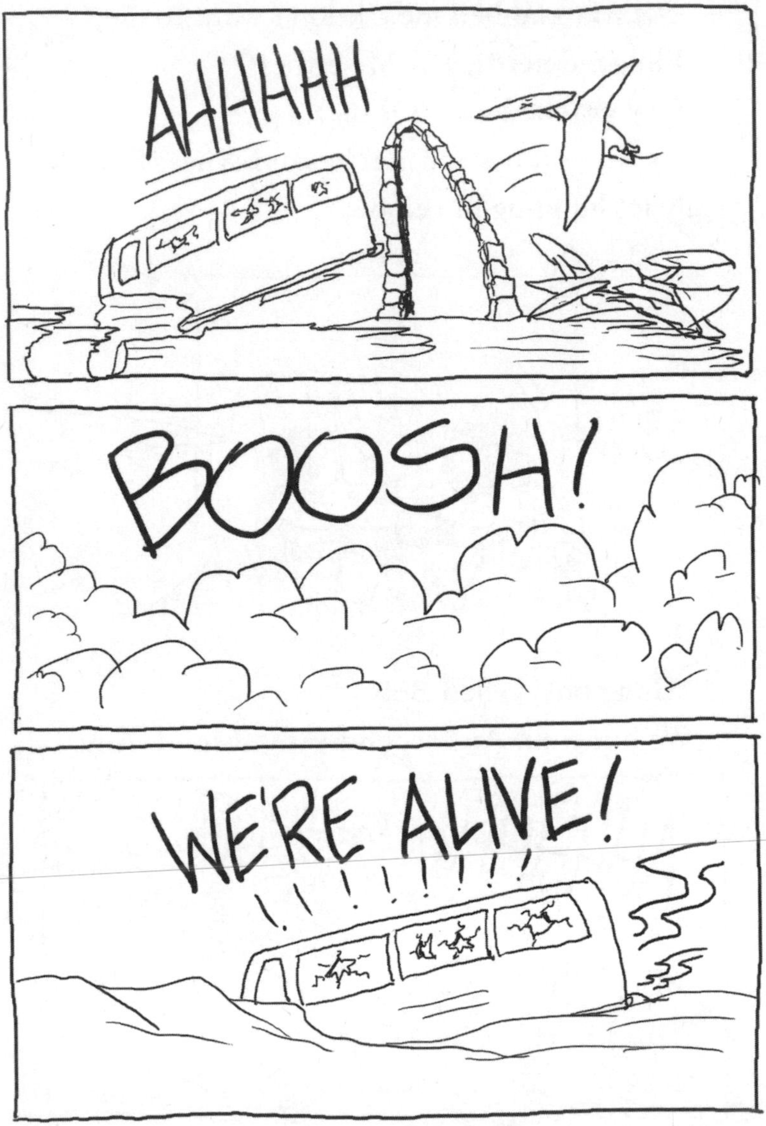
AHHHHH
BOOSH!
WE'RE ALIVE!

We really were alive. Again.

Bob shouted from the cockpit, "We've arrived!"

"Where?" I asked.

Stan explained, "The Commodore is coming back for you, kid. We need room to fight where no civilians will get hurt."

"Also, it's a friendly place," said Bob. "Where everyone's got your back."

"Friendly?" I asked.

Stan pointed out the window. "Monument Valley."

"Those rocks are your friends?" I said.

Bob said, "Just because they don't move much doesn't mean they're aren't alive."

"Hey, look, Betty's lost some weight," said Stan.

I know. I've got some really weird friends.

CHAPTER 46

We were in Monument Valley. It was certainly a cool backdrop. I mean, if you're going to have a galactic battle to save the universe, you could do worse.

STILL NO BARS! WHY CAN'T WE SAVE THE UNIVERSE SOMEWHERE THERE'S CELL RECEPTION?

Some of the other supers were already there and others kept arriving.

In short order, all the supers congregated on the valley floor. It was quite a sight—heroes and villains, super supers and lame supers...everyone was ready to fight. That's when it hit me. What are we fighting for?

Octavia stepped forward. "You're cute. But, no. We're fighting for ourselves. When one of us is attacked, *all* of us are attacked."

Whoa. She thinks I'm cute.

I said, "Captain Chaos and the Commodore just want me. I could just surrender and all of you could go on about your super lives."

"You can't trust the Commodore to do that," said Niles. "And we don't want you to sacrifice yourself for us."

We? Who body-snatched Niles?

Javy raised his hand. "But if you're right and the Smear is on our side, then this could be our one chance to destroy the Commodore so we're all safe."

"But what if I'm wrong?" I said. "I've been wrong before. I'll probably be wrong again."

My mom said, "You asked us to trust you, so we're trusting you."

"I'm really not kidding about the librarian thing," I said.

"We know," said Dad. "We've always known."

Mom added, "When this is all over, you can do whatever you want. You will have earned it."

Okay. Maybe I won't divorce them after all.

I stood there for a moment. It's a really big deal when people put their faith in you. It can either fill you with confidence or crush you with doubt. Or in my case, you try to do everything in your power to earn their faith.

That felt good.

"What's next?" I said.

Bob and Stan lumbered up. "We're going to use you as bait to lure the Commodore into an ambush. When he comes to kidnap you, we'll strike."

"Me? Bait?" I asked.

"Bait," said Bob.

GULP!

CHAPTER 47

Waiting.

Waiting.

Waiting.

Waiting for the next part of my life to begin.

Or end. Or get really, really messy.

In a few seconds, or minutes, or hours, or days (I hope it's not days—that would really stink), the final battle for the survival of the supers would begin. And the irony is we're about to fight a fake super that *we* created. A robot super.

Are we all going to be replaced by robots?

Man, that would really stink, too.

When you're waiting for the rest of your life to start (or end), you start thinking about weird stuff. Like, is this what I really want to keep doing? Fighting...battling...It used to be all fake and kind of fun. Now it's for real. And, to be honest, still kind of fun. I mean, if you survive.

But I really am serious about the librarian thing. Librarians hardly ever fight robots or Commodores or giant hamsters. At least, I don't think they do. But then again, what do I know about being a librarian? Maybe there's a lot more stuff going on behind the shelves than I know about.

And maybe, just maybe, if I did become a librarian, all I'd think about is being here.

Waiting.

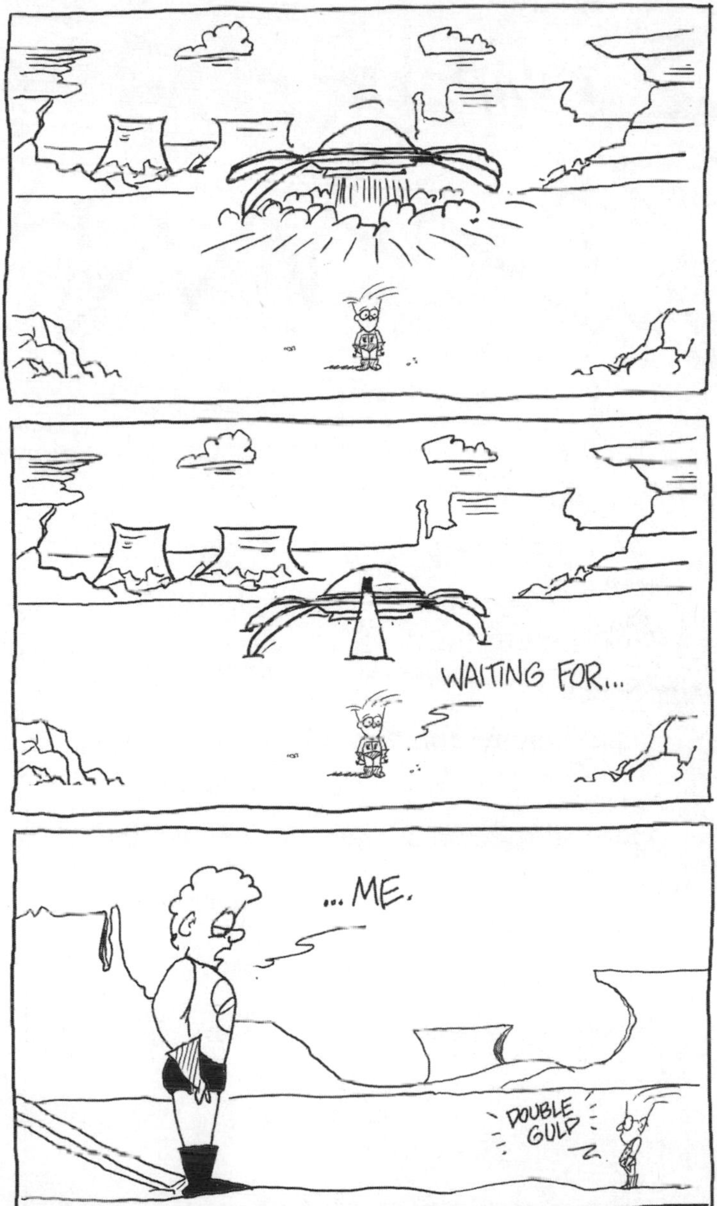
WAITING FOR...
...ME.
DOUBLE GULP

CHAPTER 48

I turned around to face Captain Chaos. "Smear, is that you inside?"

"Yes," he replied.

"Why are you attacking us?" I asked.

"It's time to finish this once and for all," said the Smear.

"The Commodore is making you do this, isn't he?"

He stared down at me. "No one is making me do anything."

"You came to take me away?"

"No," he said. "I came to battle."

I nodded. "Then you came to the right place."

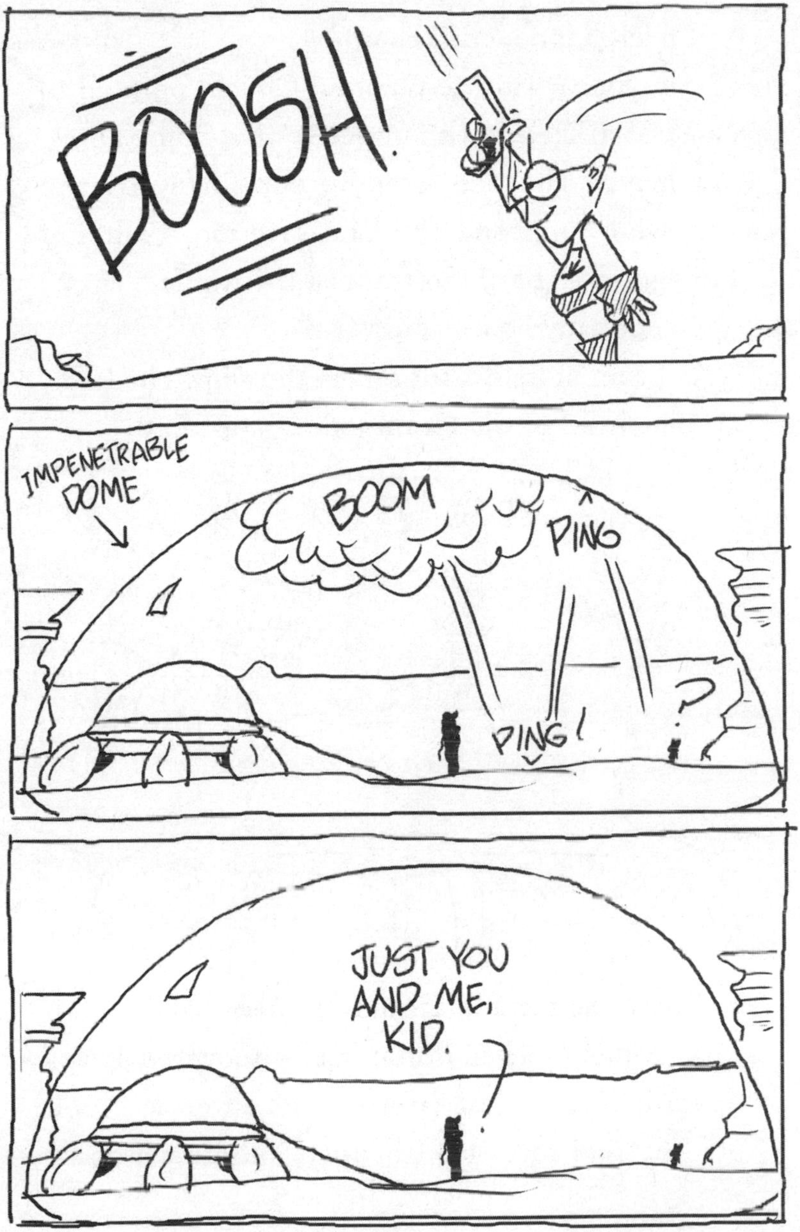
BOOSH!
IMPENETRABLE DOME
BOOM
PING
PING!
?
JUST YOU AND ME, KID.

"What happened?" I said.

The Smear (inside Captain Chaos) pointed to cameras affixed to the impenetrable dome above our heads. The one keeping out all my friends who were supposed to come save me. "You and I are going to battle in front of the whole galaxy."

I shook my head. "No way."

A beam of light shot out of the ship. The holographic head of the Commodore appeared.

I TOLD YOU I'D BE BACK!

BACK TO FEATURE THE BIGGEST BATTLE IN THE GALAXY! RIGHT HERE! RIGHT NOW!

The Smear made Captain Chaos take a step toward me. "The Commodore discovered I was operating the robot pretty soon after we took off," he told me. "He got mad and demanded I

292

help him capture you again. There was no way I was going to cooperate until the Commodore made me an offer I couldn't refuse."

"Fight the battle and then all Earth's supers go free," the Commodore explained. "No life and death galactic gladiator battles. No being frozen into uncomfortable action poses."

"They'd all go free?" I asked.

"Totally free," said the Commodore.

"And if I refuse?" I asked.

"Then I take *all* of you on the road with me."

I turned to tell the supers to escape, but it was too late.

Terrific. Now everybody was trapped.

The Commodore said, "We were going to grab you and fight the battle back on the island, but we didn't anticipate your very clever mud pie attack. No matter. This is a much more dramatic backdrop for...

The Smear said, "Lame. I know."

I agreed. "The lamest."

"It's all for the greater good," said the Smear.

"Except the greater good doesn't include us," I pointed out.

"Not this time," the Smear agreed.

I addressed the Commodore. "This isn't going to be much of a battle. You've got the greatest robot super ever created versus, you know, the Tickler."

The Commodore smiled pleasantly. "You're going to do everything you can to kill Captain Chaos. If you don't fight for your life like you did in the Bostocalypse, I'll never let the supers go."

"More threats," I said.

The Commodore nodded to the cameras. "I have a galaxy to entertain."

"You can do it, Victor," encouraged the Smear. "Remember, it's not the superpower..."

"Yeah, yeah," I said. "It's the power of the super."

"One more thing," said the Smear.

"There's more?" I said.

"The winner gets pie."

I turned and looked outside the dome.

CHAPTER 49

The Smear and I had fought together in Des Moines against MegaMole and in Fargo against Catman Fu. But we'd never fought against each other and never in front of the whole galaxy.

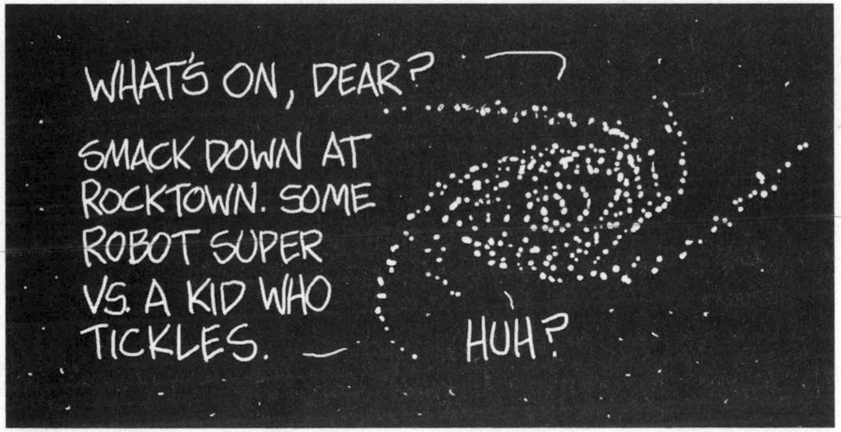
WHAT'S ON, DEAR?
SMACK DOWN AT ROCKTOWN. SOME ROBOT SUPER VS. A KID WHO TICKLES.
HUH?

It was quite a production. If I wasn't fighting

for my life, I'd be impressed. We had robot squirrel announcers…

GALACTIC SPORTS

…robot squirrel cheerleaders…

...and robot squirrel Brad as the referee.

I DON'T WANT TO SEE ANY HOLDING BACK. I DON'T WANT TO SEE ANY PITY. AND I CERTAINLY DON'T WANT TO SEE ANY SPORTSMANSHIP...

"I'm sorry about this," said the Smear inside Captain Chaos.

DING! DING! DING!

WE'RE CIRCLING

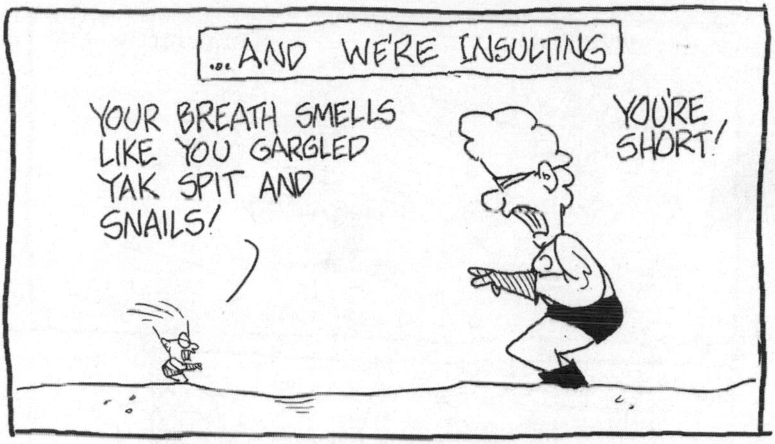
...AND WE'RE INSULTING
YOUR BREATH SMELLS LIKE YOU GARGLED YAK SPIT AND SNAILS!
YOU'RE SHORT!

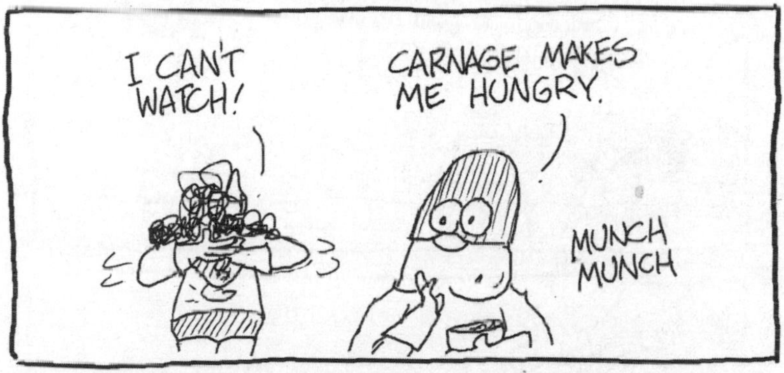
I CAN'T WATCH!
CARNAGE MAKES ME HUNGRY.
MUNCH MUNCH

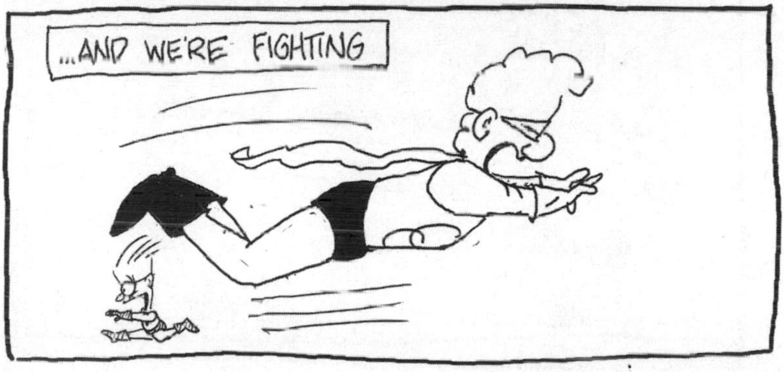
...AND WE'RE FIGHTING

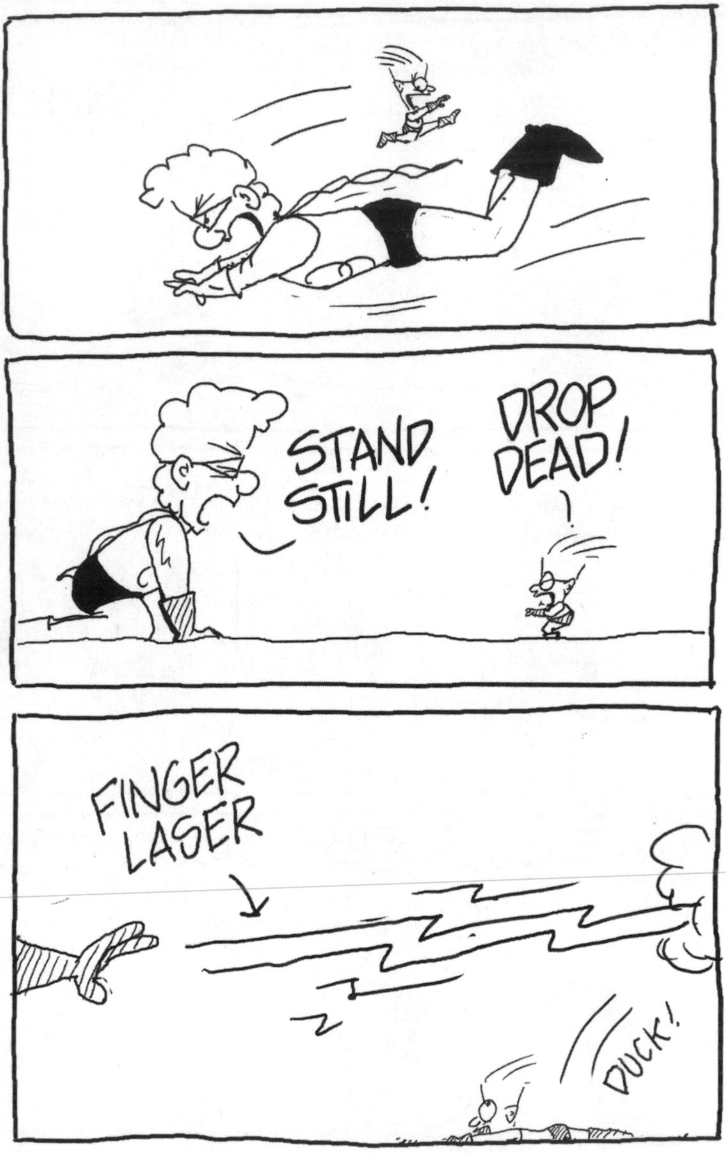
STAND STILL!
DROP DEAD!
FINGER LASER
DUCK!

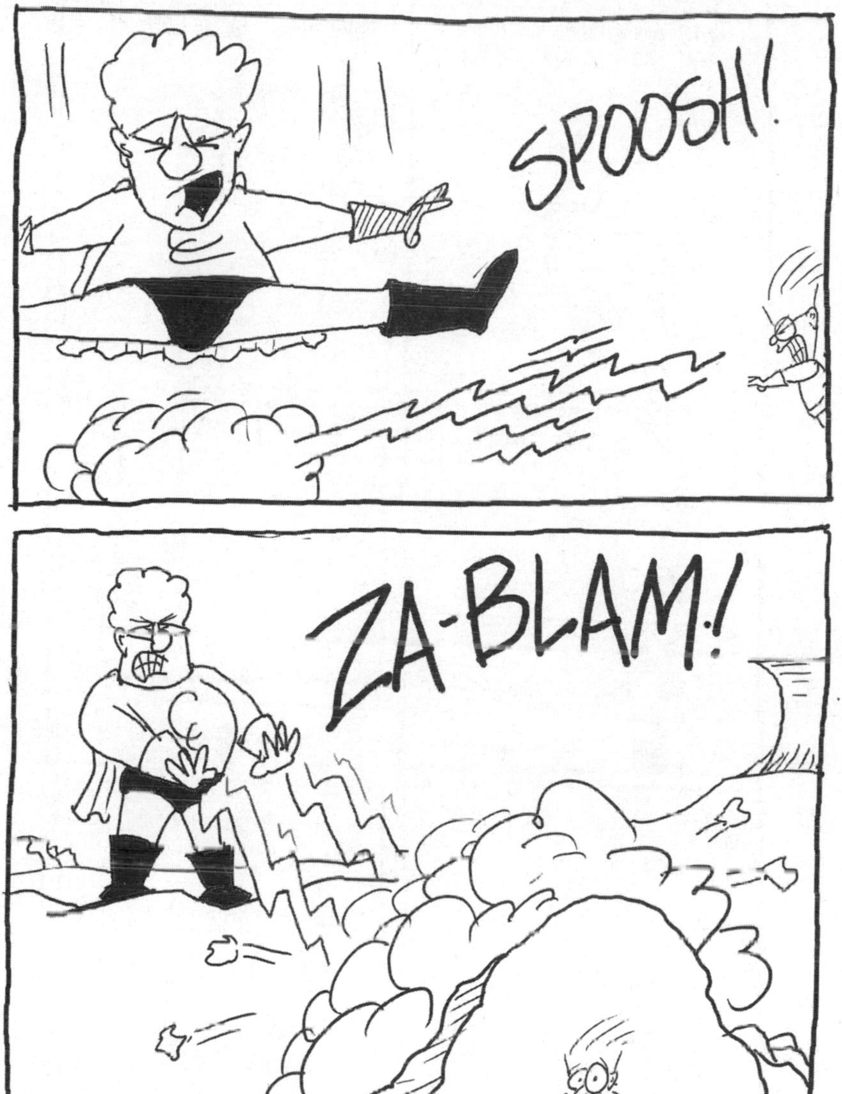
SPOOSH!
ZA-BLAM!

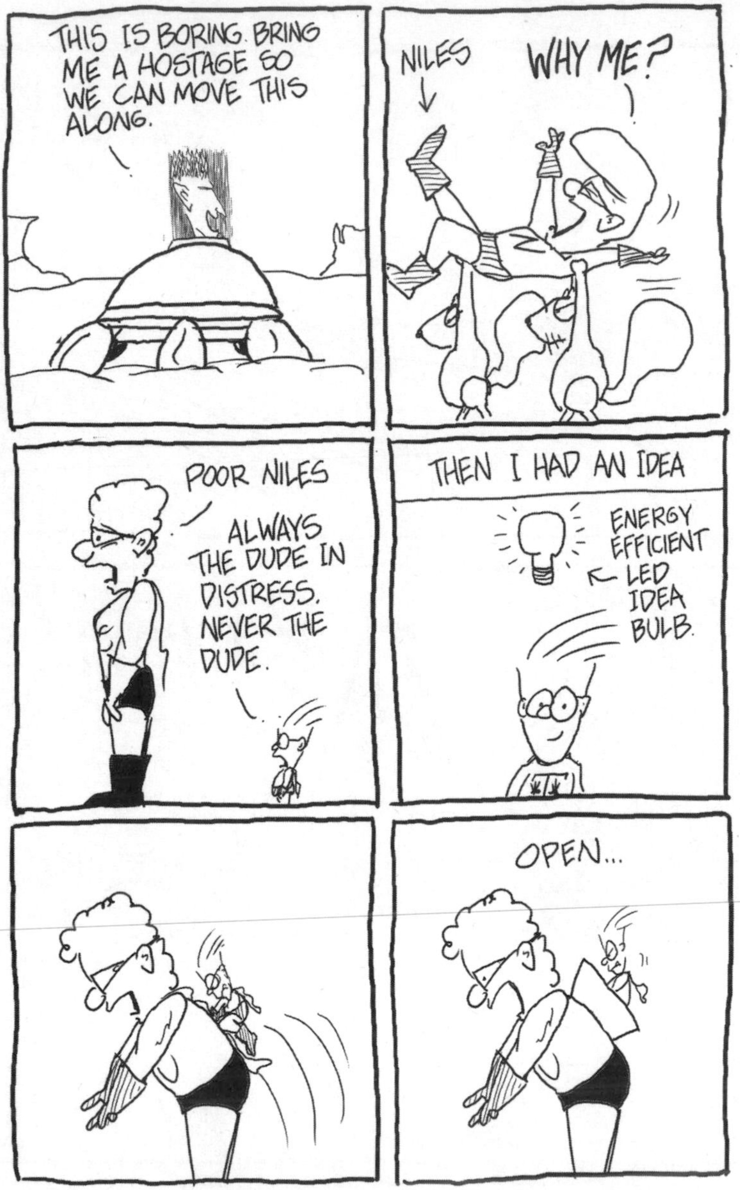
THIS IS BORING. BRING ME A HOSTAGE SO WE CAN MOVE THIS ALONG.
NILES
WHY ME?
POOR NILES
ALWAYS THE DUDE IN DISTRESS. NEVER THE DUDE.
THEN I HAD AN IDEA
ENERGY EFFICIENT LED IDEA BULB.
OPEN...

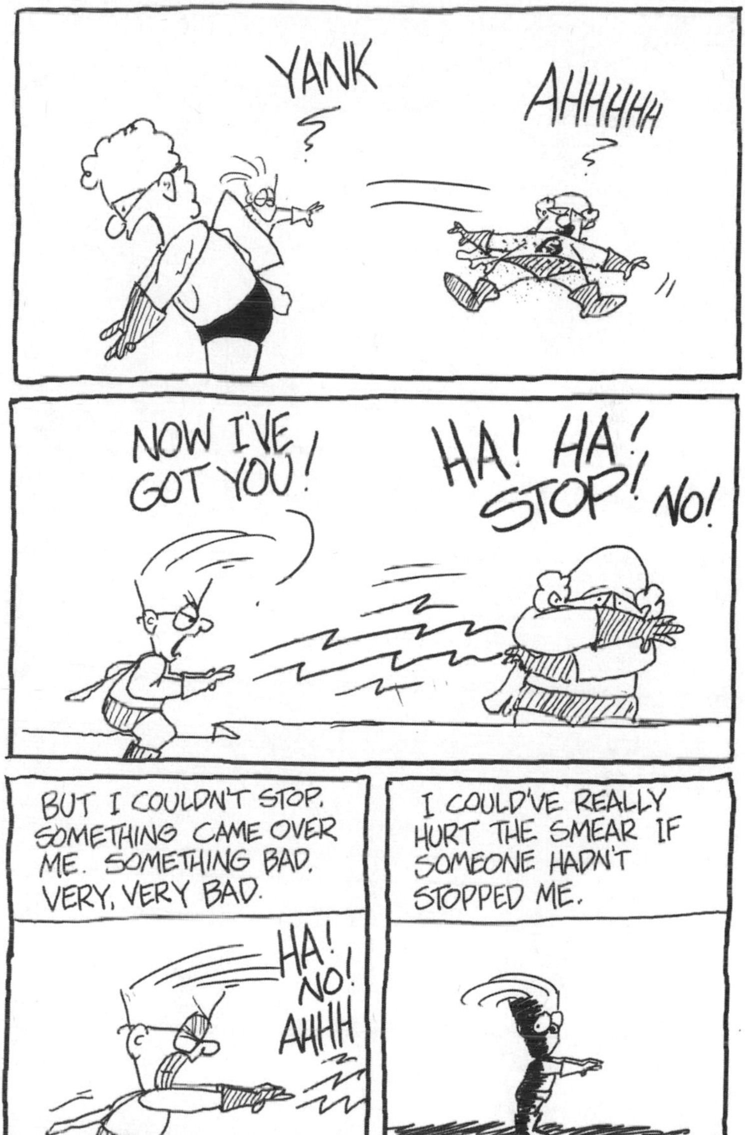
YANK
AHHHHH
NOW I'VE GOT YOU!
HA! HA! STOP! NO!
BUT I COULDN'T STOP. SOMETHING CAME OVER ME. SOMETHING BAD. VERY, VERY BAD.
HA! NO! AHHH
I COULD'VE REALLY HURT THE SMEAR IF SOMEONE HADN'T STOPPED ME.

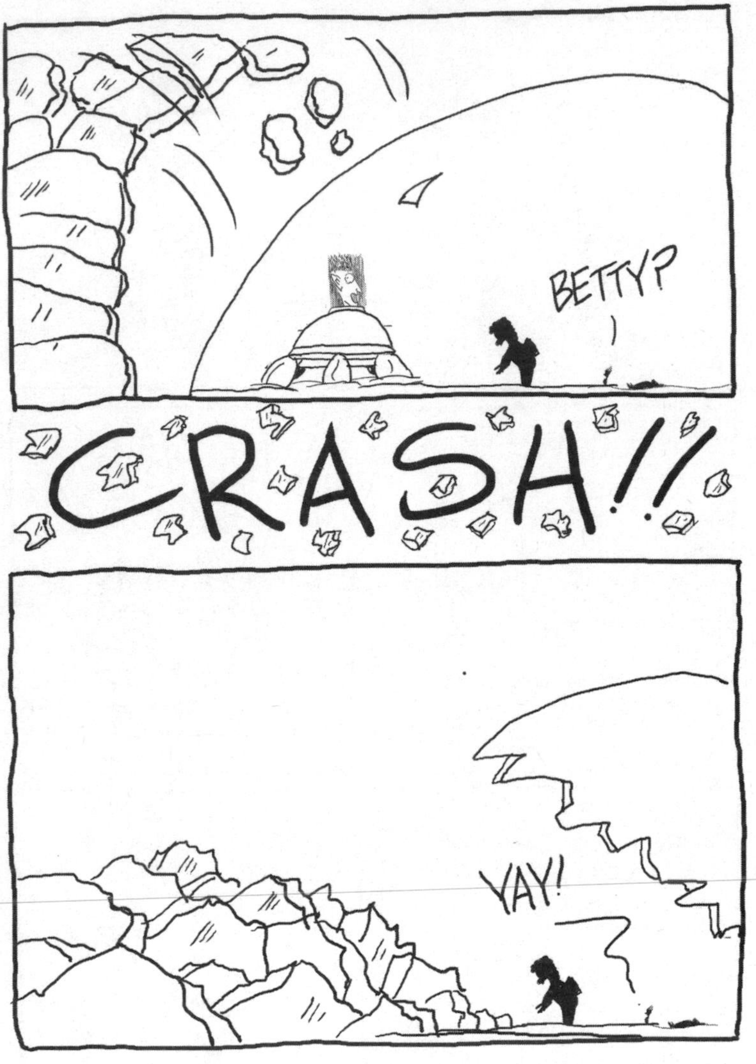
BETTY?
CRASH!!
YAY!

I said, “Me too.”

CHAPTER 50

"What was that?" said the Smear.

"It's Betty to the rescue!" I cried.

Betty the rock monster had tipped herself over and fallen, crushing both domes and releasing the Smear and me and all the supers.

"Bob and Stan said she was alive," I said. "But I didn't believe them."

"I have no idea what you're talking about," said the Smear.

"It doesn't matter...

WE'RE ALIVE!!

BARELY...

PANT PANT

"You were going to stop with the tickling, right?" asked the Smear. "I mean, at some point."

"Of course!" I said.

But in my head, I was panicking. *What the heck just happened there? I wasn't in control. I could have hurt him. Like with Niles, back at school. What's wrong with me? I'm not evil. Or am I?*

Before I could figure it all out, I turned to see my parents and Octavia running toward us.

We made it! I can't believe we survived. Thank the rock monsters...and their friends.

Wow. So, that was, you know, *insane*. Me and the Smear going full smackdown to save the supers.

What next?

Captain Chaos coming back to life and busting some awesome hip-hop dance moves?

I hate it when I'm half right.

"Wait," yelled the Smear. "Is that the Commodore's voice?"

It was. The Commodore had taken over Captain Chaos!

"You're going down," the Commodore said as Captain Chaos's eye lasers surged with power.

"Everyone take cover!" I cried.

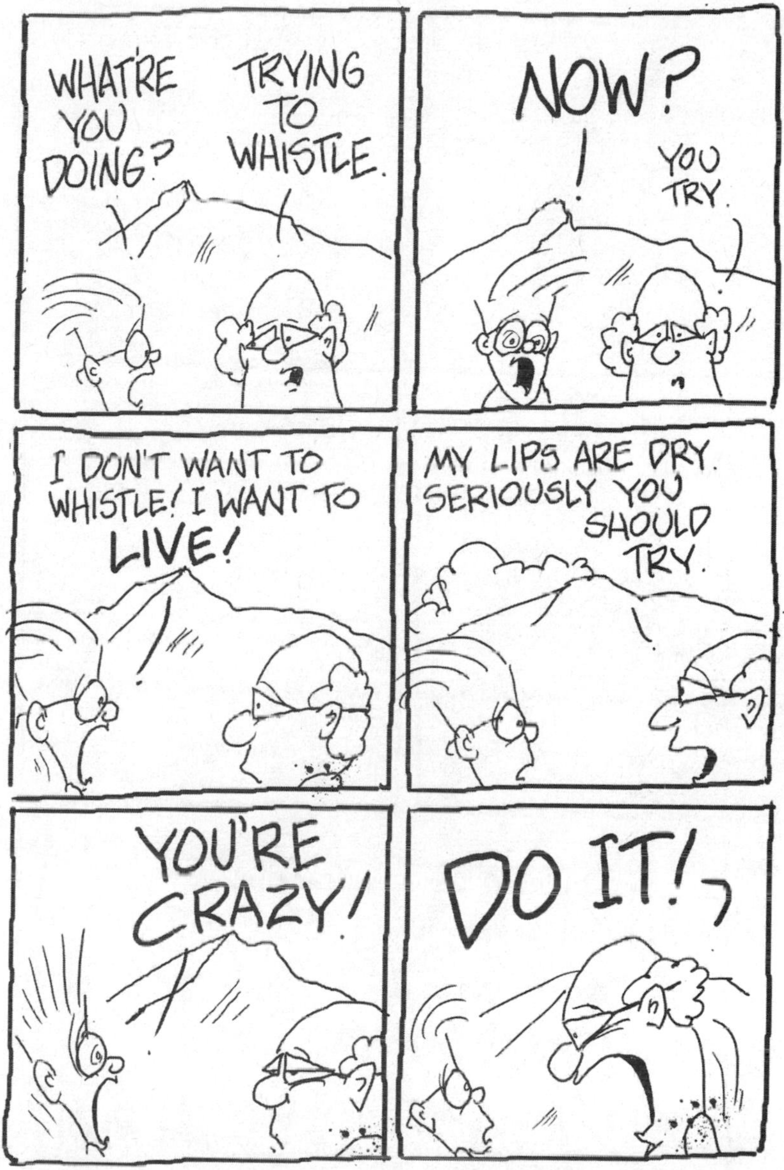
WHAT'RE YOU DOING?
TRYING TO WHISTLE.
NOW?
YOU TRY.
I DON'T WANT TO WHISTLE! I WANT TO LIVE!
MY LIPS ARE DRY. SERIOUSLY YOU SHOULD TRY.
YOU'RE CRAZY!
DO IT!

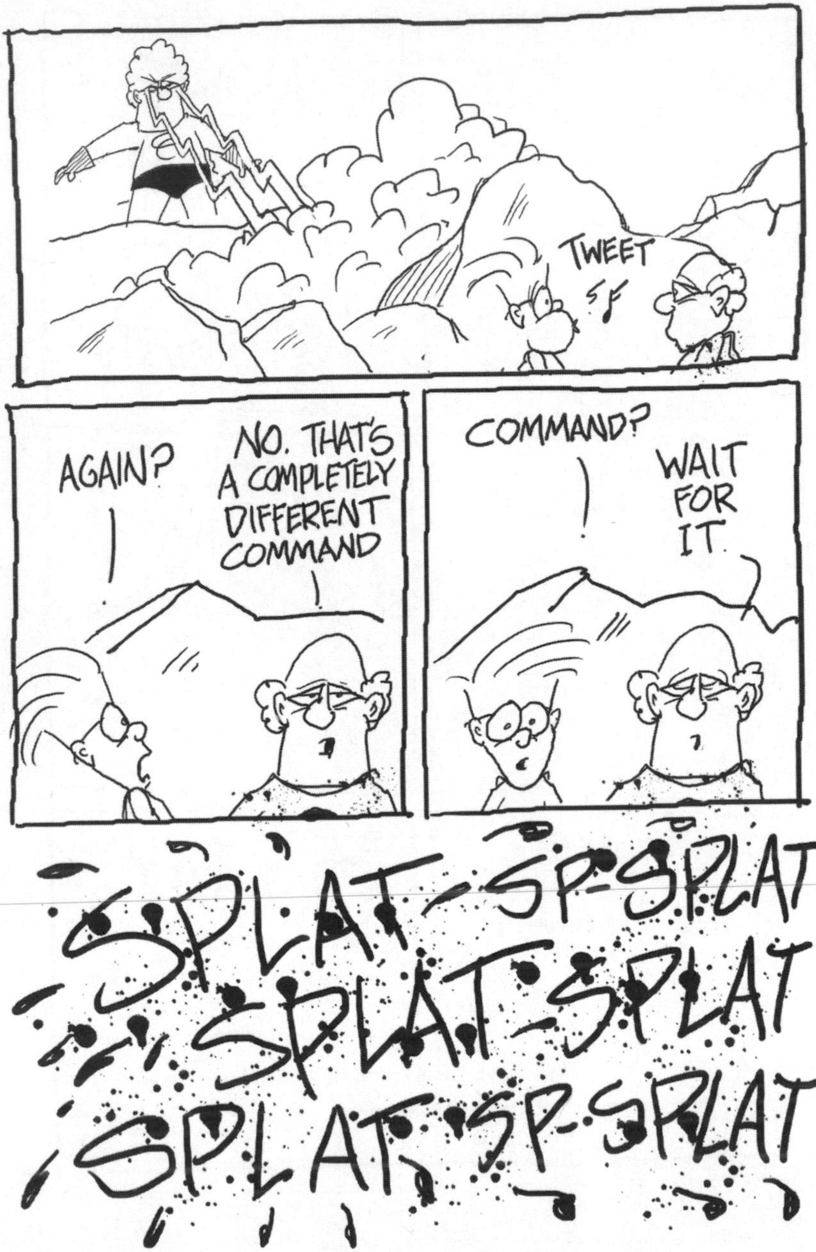
TWEET
AGAIN?
NO. THAT'S A COMPLETELY DIFFERENT COMMAND
COMMAND?
WAIT FOR IT
SPLAT-SP-SPLAT
SPLAT-SPLAT
SPLAT SP-SPLAT

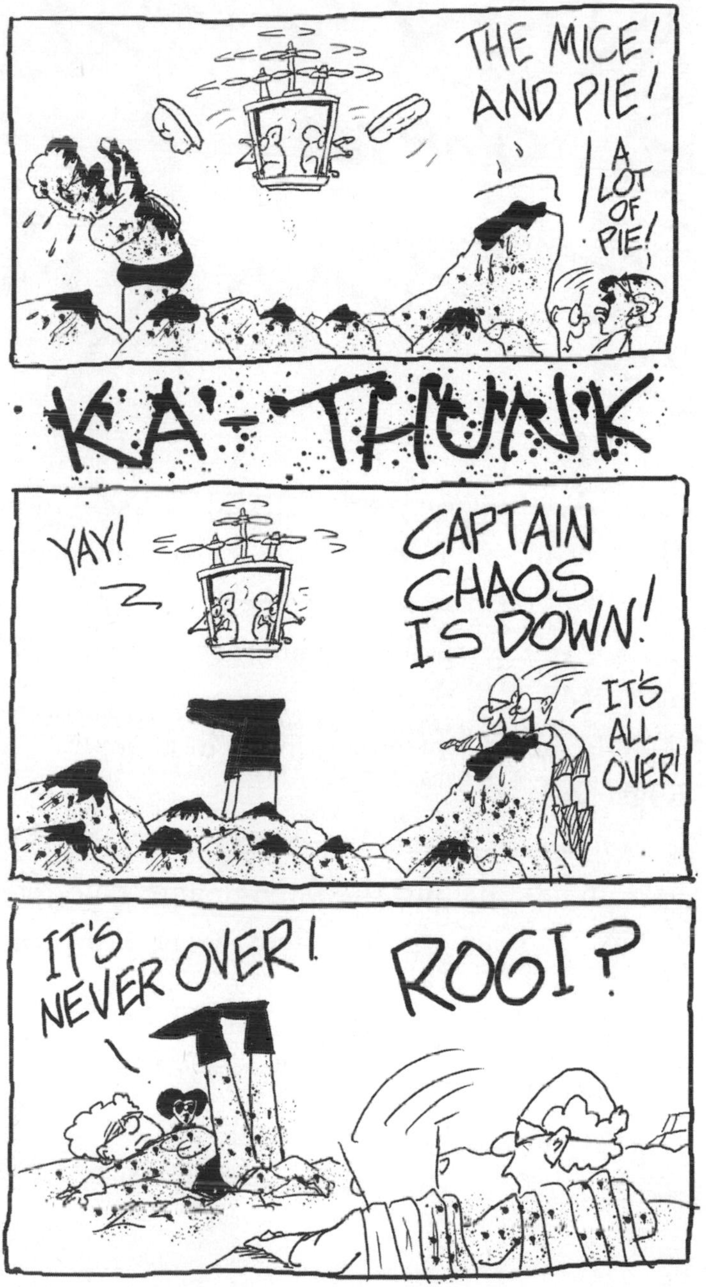
THE MICE! AND PIE!
A LOT OF PIE!
KA-THUNK
YAY!
CAPTAIN CHAOS IS DOWN!
IT'S ALL OVER!
IT'S NEVER OVER!
ROGI?

CHAPTER 51

Rogi, aka the Commodore, tried to back away. The Smear and I and all the supers, great and lame, cautiously approached her.

"So, you were the Commodore all along," I marveled.

"Of course! I've always been in charge," said Rogi.

"I'm disappointed," said Octavia. "You didn't have to hide behind the Commodore hologram thingy. I mean you're plenty scary on your own."

"Thank you," said Rogi.

"You're welcome," said Octavia.

I eyed Rogi. "Ready to give up?"

Why do bad guys (including bad women) never give up? She's surrounded. Her ship is demolished. She has no weapons. She's toast. Nevertheless...

...she persists.

"Okay," I said. "We need some intel on this lady. Javy?"

Javy raised his hand. "Present!"

I said, "Javy, get in her head and find out what her superproblem is."

"In her head?" asked Javy. "What if there are spiders?"

I glared at Javy. "You know what I mean."

Javy closed his eyes and tried to concentrate. Which looked a lot like a squid trying to yodel.

"Whoa," said Javy.

"What?" I said.

Javy said, "She really hates cheese."

"Concentrate!" I growled.

Javy continued, "Oh. Right. Okay. I've got it."

"What?" I asked.

"She's jealous," said Javy.

"*Jealous?*" said Octavia incredulously.

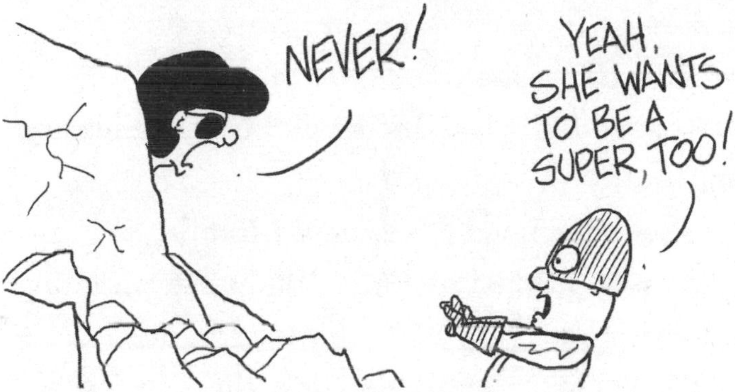

NEVER!
YEAH, SHE WANTS TO BE A SUPER, TOO!

"That's it?" I said. "All of this…this *insanity* was because you want to be like us?"

"M-maybe just a little," Rogi stammered. "You're invincible."

"Are you kidding me?" I yelled. "You made us fight each other to the death!"

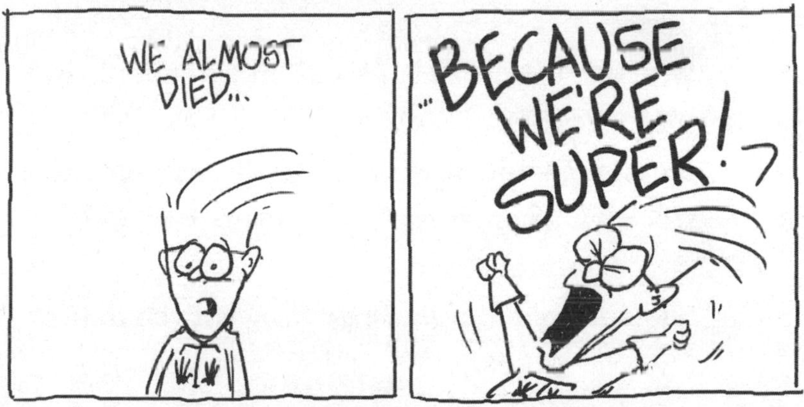

WE ALMOST DIED...
...BECAUSE WE'RE SUPER!

"But you didn't," said Rogi.

"Because we're super," said the Smear.

I said, "We're doomed if we are and doomed if we aren't."

"Something like that," said the Smear.

Mom added, "You'd miss all this at the library, son."

I shook my head. "Not now, Mom."

Octavia pointed at Rogi. "What are we going to do with her?"

"We could catapult her into the sun," Niles suggested.

"We could make her eat cheese," said Javy.

"We could make her read about strong, empowered women like Helen Keller and Eleanor Roosevelt," declared Octavia.

"Or..." said the Smear. "We could give her a superpower."

"WHAT?" I cried. "That seems like a super bad idea."

"Trust me," said the Smear, as he pointed to the still-rolling cameras. "I play a supervillain on TV."

"Shouldn't she be punished for what she did?"

I asked. "Giving her a superpower is like rewarding her bad behavior."

The Smear looked at me. "Remember what I always say?"

Right. The power of the super. I realized that without the holographic head, the tractor beam, and the threats, Rogi didn't have much power at all. And the Smear asked me to trust him. Even after trying to destroy me.

Did I?

I took a deep breath. Then I nodded.

"You're going to give me a superpower?" said Rogi. "How? What's the catch?"

The Smear smiled. "You'll see."

The Smear turned to Bob and Stan, who were just that instant exiting the space bus holding several bottles of a dark golden liquid. "Hey, guys? Just a second. Can you please hand those over?"

"Hand what over?" said Bob.

"The Nilaxian root beer," said the Smear.

Stan said, "No. This is, you know, just, you know, iced tea."

The Smear barked. "Hand it over!"

The rock monsters complied. Reluctantly.

"Wait," I said. "That's that stuff they smuggle. That stuff that gives you superpowers by taking your biggest weakness and making it your biggest strength."

"That's right," said the Smear.

Then, ever so slowly, Rogi approached me. She put her arms out and...

I turned to the Smear. "Fandom is her super-power?"

"The Nilaxian root beer turned her jealousy into awe," said the Smear. "We like awe."

The Smear said, "It's harmless. And now she's harmless. It's like I keep saying, 'It's not the superpower...'"

Got it?
Good.

EPILOGUE

The Smear and I watched as Rogi asked Javy to autograph her forehead.

"Yeah, this is definitely going to get old," I said.

The Smear asked, "So, you're really going to quit all this and become a librarian?"

"Maybe," I said.

The Smear said, "You could be a librarian *and* a supervillain. You could be one of those supers who has a civilian job where no one recognizes you're a supervillain even though the only difference is you wear glasses in your civilian job. You know, like FabDude."

"No one's really fooled, are they?" I asked.

The Smear said, "You'd be surprised. Civilians see what they want to see."

"Good," said the Smear, as we walked over to the deactivated Captain Chaos.

I said, "Hey, he might hear you."

"Victor, Captain Chaos is a piloted robot. He can't hear us. He doesn't have feelings."

"How do you know that for sure?"

"Watch."

I stared at Captain Chaos. Is he more than just a robot? There's something about his eyes.

They're like that Mona Lisa painting. They follow you everywhere.

Nah. That's ridiculous. He's just a robot. But if you think about it, he's *my* robot since I made him up, which makes him special. At least to me.

"Can we keep him?" I asked the Smear.

"What're you going to use him for?" asked the Smear.

Hmm...I had to think about that.

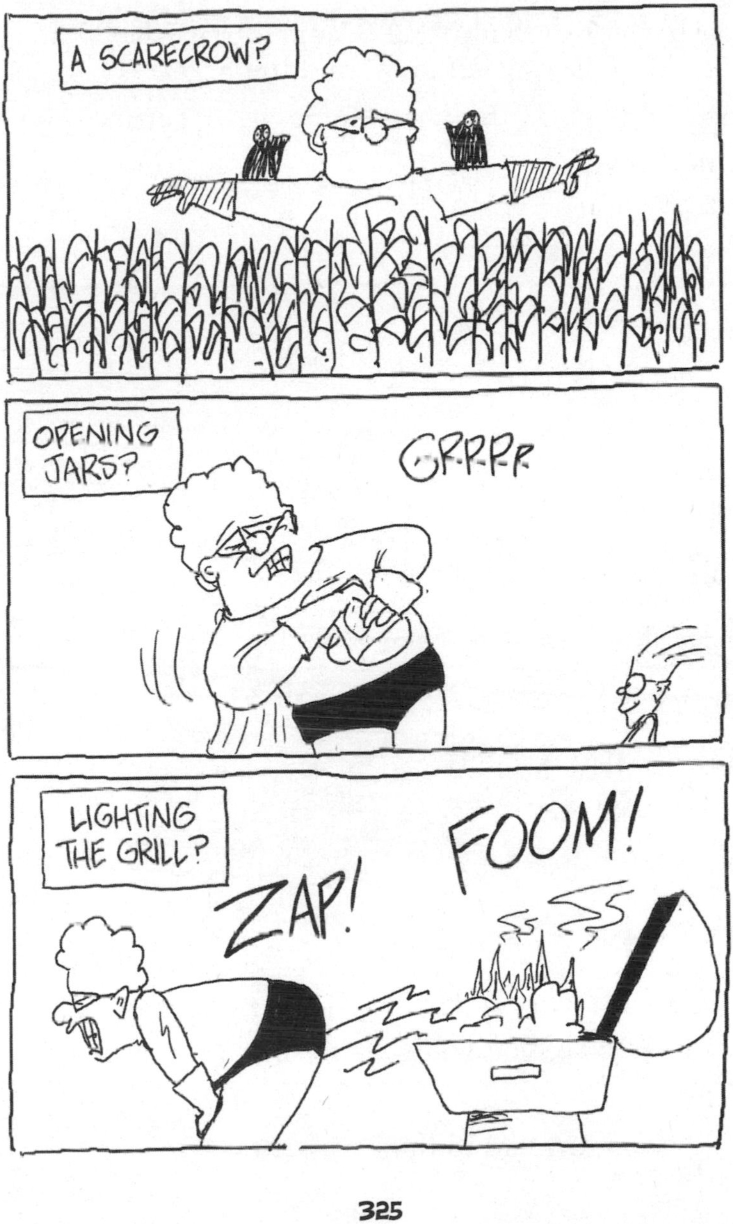
A SCARECROW?
OPENING JARS?
GRPPP
LIGHTING THE GRILL?
FOOM!
ZAP!

I said, "I don't know. I'll find a use for him."

"Knock yourself out," said the Smear.

"I'm going to need some help getting him home."

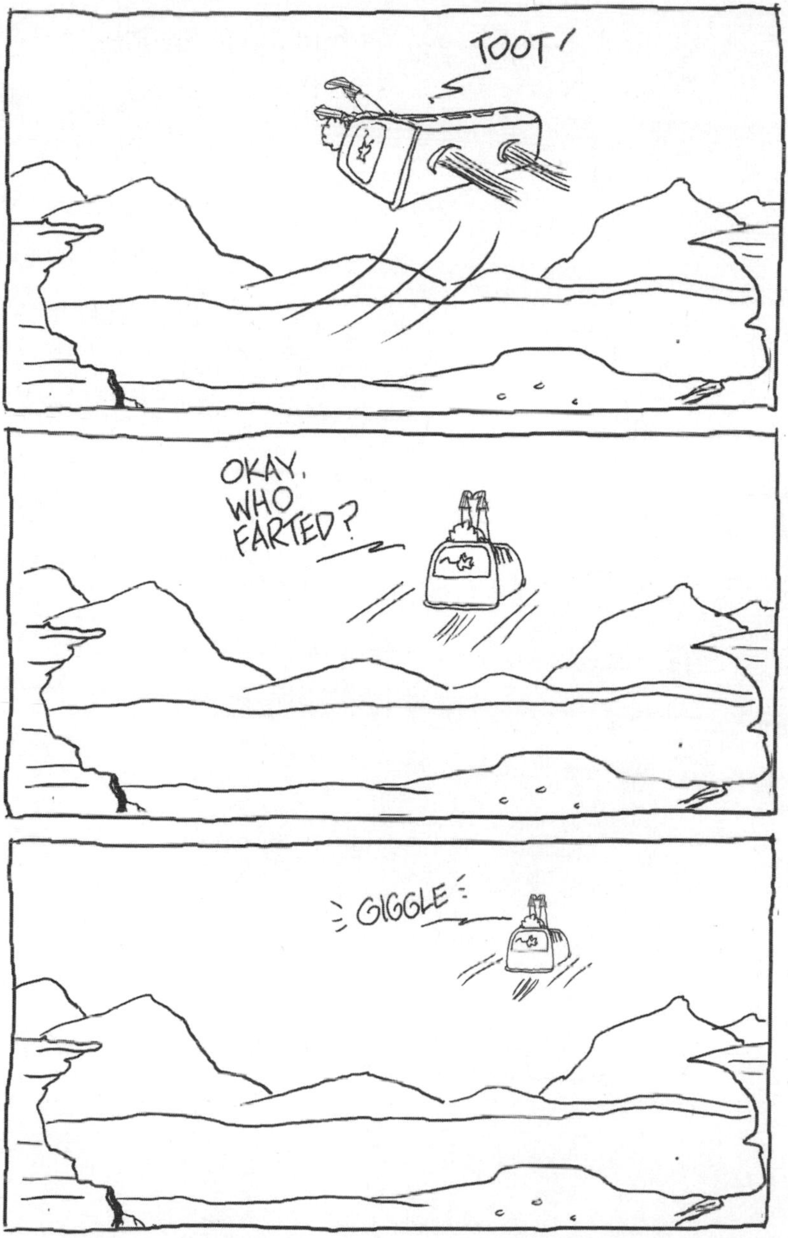
TOOT!
OKAY. WHO FARTED?
GIGGLE

IF YOU LIKED THIS STORY, CHECK OUT MY FIRST BOOK!

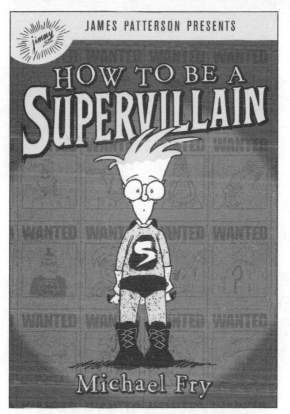

IT'S WICKED GOOD!
TURN THE PAGE
FOR A SNEAK PEEK.

PROLOGUE

My parents used to fight a lot.

Wait. No. Not with each other. They used to fight other people for a living.

Yup. My parents are supers. Supervillains, to be exact. Meet Rupert and Olivia Spoil, otherwise known as...

I know. Pretty lame. But it works for them. Not so much for me.

Let me explain. My name is Victor Spoil. I'm twelve years old and I was raised to be bad.

Which is a problem...

...when you're actually good.

CHAPTER 1

Look at me.

ME.

ME BEING BAD.

TINY TONGUE STICKING OUT

More than lame.

I mean, I try to be bad. Seriously, I do. But it's harder than it looks.

Being bad requires a lack of imagination. You can't allow yourself to imagine what might happen if you do a bad thing.

You have to not care.

You have to not care that your space plane takes up three parking spots. You have to not care that no one appreciates having their car crushed by the overpass that collapses after your Disintegrator Ray misfires. You have to not care that evildoing is very messy and those grass stains on your supersuit are really hard to get out.

I can't do that.

I can't *not* care.

I've tried. Really, I have. I tried running with scissors.

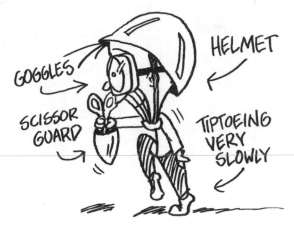

GOGGLES

HELMET

SCISSOR GUARD

TIPTOEING VERY SLOWLY

But I'm not the most coordinated kid and I just hate to make a mess.

I tried not eating all my peas.

But I like peas. They're full of vitamin K *and* a good source of fiber.

I even tried not washing behind my ears once, but it just felt...I don't know... so very, *very* wrong.

I'm a good kid. Which, in my parents' eyes, means I'm a bad kid. But I'm not the *good* kind of bad kid. I'm the *bad* kind of good kid.

My parents try to understand. But it's hard.

It's hard on all of us.

CHAPTER **2**

I come from a long line of supervillains.

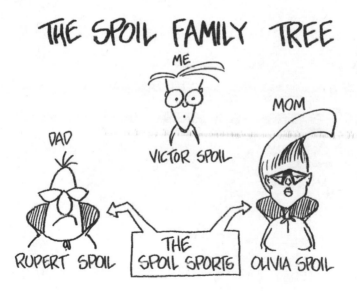

THE SPOIL FAMILY TREE

ME

VICTOR SPOIL

MOM

DAD

RUPERT SPOIL

THE SPOIL SPORTS

OLIVIA SPOIL

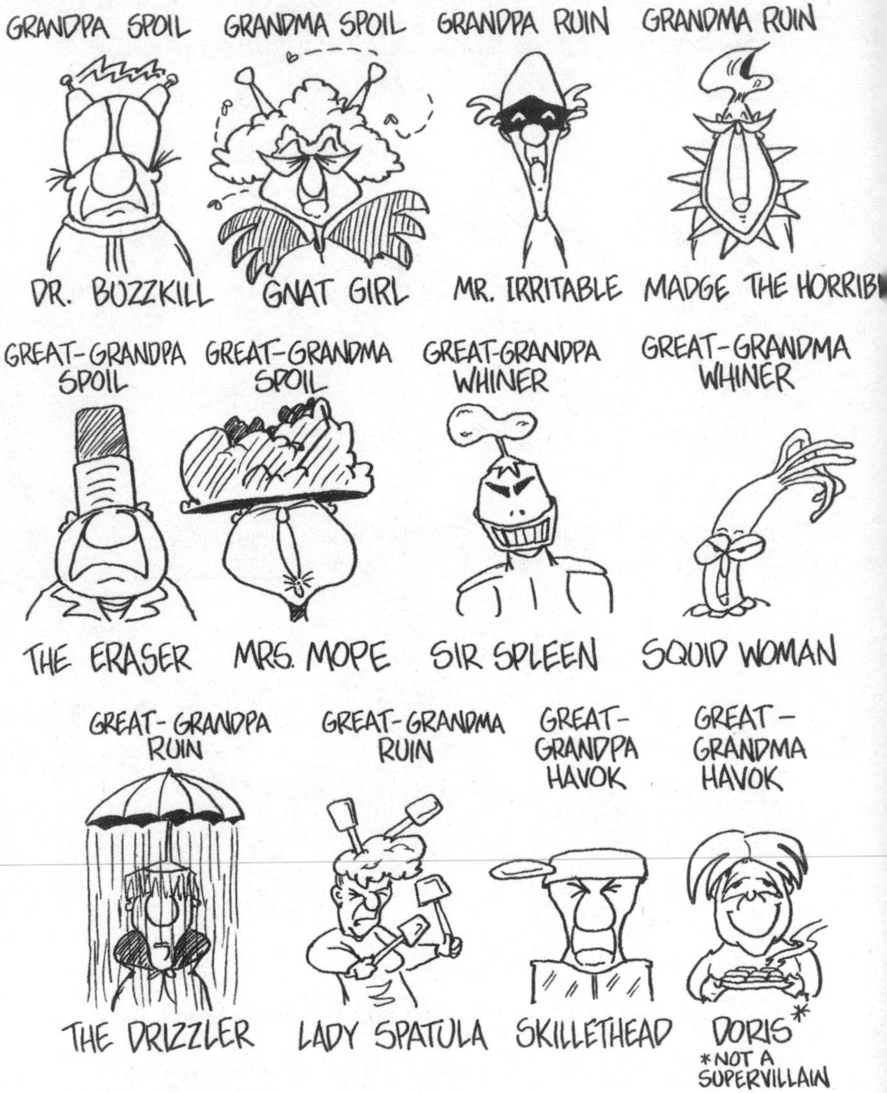
GRANDPA SPOIL
DR. BUZZKILL
GRANDMA SPOIL
GNAT GIRL
GRANDPA RUIN
MR. IRRITABLE
GRANDMA RUIN
MADGE THE HORRIB
GREAT-GRANDPA SPOIL
THE ERASER
GREAT-GRANDMA SPOIL
MRS. MOPE
GREAT-GRANDPA WHINER
SIR SPLEEN
GREAT-GRANDMA WHINER
SQUID WOMAN
GREAT-GRANDPA RUIN
THE DRIZZLER
GREAT-GRANDMA RUIN
LADY SPATULA
GREAT-GRANDPA HAVOK
SKILLETHEAD
GREAT-GRANDMA HAVOK
DORIS*
*NOT A SUPERVILLAIN

My parents are minor supervillains and pretty much semiretired. Let's call them supervillain*ish*. These days they're more into battling to take over the recliner than trying to take over the world.

Still, they want what all supervillain parents want. They want me to grow up evil, with a chip on my shoulder and a burning desire to spread chaos and mayhem across the universe.

Did I mention how much I don't like to make a mess?

So instead of a hard-charging destroyer of worlds, they got me: Tidy Boy.

Destroyer of spots.

I feel bad for Mom and Dad. Like I said, I've tried to be bad. And they've tried *everything* to help me be bad. They've tried talking to me....

They've tried punishing me....

They've tried tutors....

But nothing works. No matter what they do, they can't jump-start the bad in me. I feel bad that I can't be...you know...*bad*.

I especially felt bad that I couldn't be bad after Mom and Dad had the Talk with me.

No, not *that* Talk. The *other* Talk.

The one about how the superworld really works.

ABOUT THE AUTHOR

MICHAEL FRY has been a cartoonist for more than thirty years, and is the co-creator and writer of the *Over the Hedge* comic strip, which was turned into a DreamWorks film starring Bruce Willis and William Shatner. He lives near Austin, Texas.